COPY NO. __ __ __

# ESCAPE THIS BOOK!
## RACE TO THE MOON

This action-packed adventure is filled with amazing facts about NASA's Apollo missions to the moon, which started in the 1960s. But this is not a history book! You will encounter real historical figures throughout this adventure, but the story is inspired by many different missions all mixed up together. Dig deeper into the facts by flipping to the Escapologist Files at the back of the book!

# ESCAPE THIS BOOK!
## RACE TO THE MOON

## BY BILL DOYLE
## ILLUSTRATED BY SARAH SAX & YOU

Random House 🏠 New York

Text copyright © 2020 by William H. Doyle
Cover art and interior illustrations copyright © 2020 by Sarah Sax

All rights reserved. Published in the United States by Random House Children's Books, a division of Penguin Random House LLC, New York.

Random House and the colophon are registered trademarks of Penguin Random House LLC.

Visit us on the Web! rhcbooks.com

Educators and librarians, for a variety of teaching tools, visit us at RHTeachersLibrarians.com

Library of Congress Control Number 2020939776

ISBN 978-0-593-64660-1 (proprietary)

Printed in the United States of America
10 9 8 7 6 5 4 3 2 1

FOR THE DREAMERS, DARERS,
AND DOERS AT NASA
—B.D.

TO A.S.: FOR MILES
AND MILES AND MILES
—S.S.

Draw your face here!

Lunar modules like this one visited the moon six times from 1969 to 1972.

FOLD HERE

When you're done, fold this flap up toward you.

·1·

You are TRAPPED inside this book . . .
and this book is an Apollo mission to the moon!

In just a few pages, you'll blast off from Earth in command of a spaceflight, race across the moon in a lunar rover, or lead Mission Control to guide the crew from the ground!

Who am I? The World's Greatest Escapologist! I am in search of a helper for a very special mission. I will tell you more—including how to find me!— IF you prove yourself worthy by escaping this book.

While I am otherwise tied up, I've sent along my pet gopher, Amicus, to be my eyes and ears during your adventure. He is a master of disguise. Not as talented as I am, of course! You won't be able to see him until you draw him. I'll let you know when he's around so you can spot him.

Draw my gopher, Amicus, here!

Hello! If you get stuck in space, that's when you'll see my face!

Don't get left floating on the moon! Turn the page!

Wonder what a gopher looks like? A cross between a squirrel and a meerkat!

To survive, you'll need to *demolish*, *decide*, and *doodle* your way out. Practice your escapology with these three Quick Challenges.

# Demolish!
## Quick Challenge #1

Don't hesitate to rip, fold, and scrunch pages when I tell you to. Every second counts!

Open the hatch to this space capsule so you can climb aboard!

Tear along the dotted lines and fold the flap toward you.

Are you ready to make fast decisions as you pick your own escape path? At the back of the book, you'll find my Escapologist Files; they're jam-packed with information you'll need to get out. Flip back there when I tell you, when you see this folder, or whenever you want!

# Decide!
## Quick Challenge #2

The Saturn V rocket launched the Apollo missions into space. It was over 36 stories tall! This rocket had the most powerful engines ever built.

*Let's try out your first decision.*

*You and two other astronauts will sit here during blastoff and much of your trip.*

Turn the page.

Saturn V rocket:
363 feet

Two Statues of Liberty:
302 feet

Want to find out more about the Saturn rocket before you blast off? Flip to page 175.

PAGE 175

Or do you think you know enough already? Keep reading on the next page.

# Doodle!
## Quick Challenge #3

You'll blast off toward the moon on top of the huge Saturn V rocket—and you'll return to Earth's atmosphere in a small capsule. But your escape won't end there. You'll still need to splash down safely in the ocean.

*Your spacecraft is coming back to Earth too fast.*
*You'll smash into the water! Quick!*
*Draw a parachute here and another here to slow down your ship.*

175 miles
per hour

10,000 feet
above Earth's
surface

When you're done, fold up the flap.

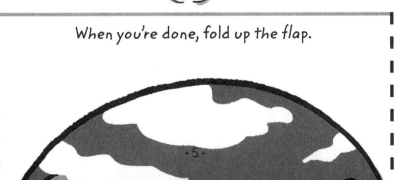

· 5 ·

Aces! You've got the basics down. Now get ready for blastoff by learning more about the Apollo program!

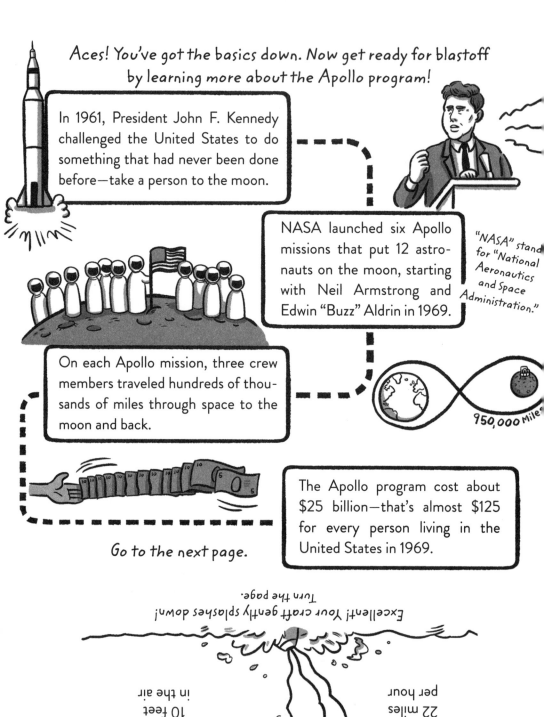

In 1961, President John F. Kennedy challenged the United States to do something that had never been done before—take a person to the moon.

NASA launched six Apollo missions that put 12 astronauts on the moon, starting with Neil Armstrong and Edwin "Buzz" Aldrin in 1969.

"NASA" stands for "National Aeronautics and Space Administration."

On each Apollo mission, three crew members traveled hundreds of thousands of miles through space to the moon and back.

950,000 Miles

The Apollo program cost about $25 billion—that's almost $125 for every person living in the United States in 1969.

Go to the next page.

Excellent! Your craft gently splashes down! Turn the page.

10 feet in the air

22 miles per hour

# Who will YOU be on this great escape?

Write your name in one of the blanks below.
I'll send you back here later to try the other paths, too!

**Difficulty Level Alert!** *Choose the paths in any order you'd like.
But beware: I've listed them here in order of trickiness—
from fairly tricky to rocket-science tricky.*

 ## MISSION COMMANDER

_____

As chief astronaut, you'll call the shots in space. Can you travel to the
moon and back by escaping one dangerous situation after another?
Blast off to page 120.

 ## MOON BUGGY DRIVER

 ## FLIGHT DIRECTOR

_____

You'll get to explore the moon
on four wheels. But first, do you
have what it takes to safely land
on the lunar surface?
Rove on over to page 68.

_____

You're the boss at Mission Control
in Houston. Can you make life-or-
death decisions in a split second?
Lead the way to page 8.

## Best of luck. (You'll need it!)

# FLIGHT DIRECTOR PATH

So you think you can guide three astronauts across thousands of miles of hostile space to a safe landing on the moon? Hmm . . . I'm not sure. First, let's see if you even know where you are!

Are you aware that you work at Mission Control? You make all the big space mission decisions and keep an eye on the spacecraft and crew 24 hours a day. The rocket that's getting ready to blast off is actually 1,000 miles away.

Prove you know how to get to Mission Control.
Go through the maze from START to FINISH. Use the
letters on your path to fill in the blanks below in order:

Mystery Phrase: ____    ____    ____    ____

When you're done, go on to the next page.

If you get stuck, flip to page 183 for help.

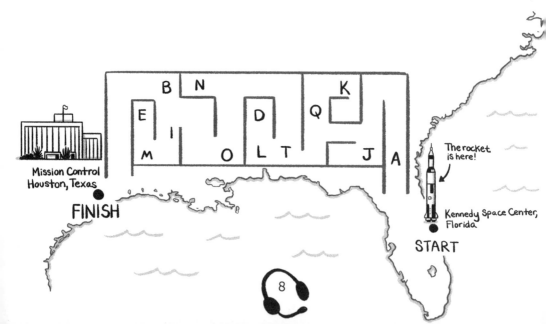

Being the flight director is all about making *big, bold* moves during a mission. You'll need to escape many traps on the way! In fact, you're in one right now—and you don't even know it.

Draw one big wavy line from ____ ____ ____ ____.

Write the Mystery Phrase here!

(A)

(B)

Draw five short, **bold** wavy lines here that look like dancing worms. I've done some for you— because I am wonderful.

When you've finished drawing, tear along the dotted line and fold the flap to find out where you are.

9

You tripped and fell into the pool where astronauts train for space missions. Not the best start to launch day, Flight Director!

Luckily, your big sister, Lynette, also works for NASA. She's standing at the side of the pool, calling your name: "Bloop bloop!"

*Hmm. Did many women work at NASA during the Apollo missions? Flip to my Escapologist Files to find out.*

PAGE 175

Bloop bloop? Is that your name? No, wait. Lynette sounds garbled because you're still underwater. When you splash to the surface, she laughs. "You always did like to *dive* into work!"

What's that floating next to you? A photo of your family came out of your pocket.

*Draw yourself in the photo! Don't forget the family pet— you named him Sputnik after the first satellite that orbited Earth, in 1957. When you're done, go to the next page.*

*You're in a swimming pool! Turn the page.*

You grab a towel and head for the door, but Lynette stops you.

"Help me with this simulation first," she says. "I want the astronauts training in the pool to feel like they're on the moon. Can you help?"

A simulation lets you act something out— like a problem that astronauts might face in space.

Well, can you?

If you add air to the astronauts' suits, they might get an idea of what it's like to walk on the moon.

PAGE 175

Which setting will you use to pump air into the astronauts' suits? Follow the line from that setting, turn over that flap, and follow the instructions.

Try again!

Well done!
Turn to page 12!

Try again!

"That worked!" Lynette says. "Now you'd better get to Mission Control. After all, it's *kind of* a big day."

*Kind of?* She's joking, of course. This is the BIGGEST day—launch day! The half-hour countdown to blastoff has started!

"I'll be here if you need me," Lynette says, patting you on the back. "Try not to fall into any more swimming pools and you'll be fine."

*I like her!*

*Now get to work—hustle to page 14.*

"Let's figure out why Alex can't dock with the lunar module," you say. "Why don't we send one of the astronauts outside the CSM to fix it?"

"That's not an option," Lynette explains. "Space suits get too stiff in the vacuum of space. Astronauts' heart rates skyrocket with effort, and they have a tough time getting back inside the spacecraft."

*Here, let me show you what Lynette means.*

1. Poke a hole here with the tip of a pen or pencil.

2. Turn your pencil or pen sideways.

3. Go through the hole.

Can't do it, right? That's how an astronaut in a stiff space suit would feel trying to get back inside the CSM.

PAGE 180

Turn to page 48.

Which capsule will reach Earth if it stays on the same path? Circle the letter and write it in blank #2 in Mission Control.

Examine the marks on this astronaut's skin—moon fever or just pimples? Either way, connect the dots. What letter did you form? Write it in blank #1 in Mission Control.

# WELCOME TO MISSION CONTROL

## ROCKET CONTROLLER

This tech keeps the engines firing correctly and the spacecraft moving in the right direction. Tear along this line and fold over this flap to give the job a try.

## FLIGHT SURGEON

This doctor tracks the crew's health!

PAGE 176

Fold over this flap to try out your medical skills.

A small group of flight controllers work here—and about 400,000 engineers, technicians, scientists, and others help from around the world. You're the flight director— the boss of all of them!

PAGE 175

To really blast off with NASA, first give these four jobs a shot. Tear along the dotted lines and fold over the four flaps, one by one. When you've completed all four activities, you'll have the word you need to complete the directions.

TURN TO PAGE

TWENTY- ___ ___ ___ ___
         1    2    3    4

Need help?
Turn to page 183.

15

# CAPSULE COMMUNICATOR

The CAPCOM is usually a trained astronaut who knows space jargon and can pass along tricky info to the crew.

PAGE 177

Fold over this flap to try out the job.

# SYSTEMS CHECK

From computers to temperature controls, you need to know the ship's electronics inside and out. Fold over this flap!

Write the last letter of this note
in blank #4 in Mission Control.

 **OUT   4**

**SP +**  **FROM**

 **-T   + OTHER**

Turn on these switches

by circling them. Your circles will
make the shape of a letter. Write it
in blank #3 in Mission Control!

16

Um, have you ever tried to be king of space with a pterodactyl flying around? Let me tell you from personal experience, your reign won't last.

# END

I **dino** about you, but I'd love to try a different ending.
Return to page 24.

Ugh! You've stacked up the three astronauts into some kind of pretzel pyramid. And Neil Armstrong just twisted his ankle!

It'll be pretty hard for him to walk on the moon like that. Time to abort the mission!

# END

Let's go for a different plot **twist**! Return to page 119.

"We have liftoff!" Chuck crows, and everyone cheers.

*Just barely,* you think as you watch the rocket on the big screen.

Even with 7.75 million pounds of thrust under it, the 6.2 million-pound rocket doesn't just zoom off into the sky right away. The heavy rocket hardly seems to be moving. In fact, it takes a whole 15 seconds for the rocket to clear the tower.

*To get an idea of how heavy 6.2 million pounds is, draw a baby African elephant blasting off from this platform.*

How many baby African elephants would you have to draw to equal the weight of just one Saturn V rocket?

At least 26,000? Turn to page 29.
Fewer than 150? Go to page 23.

Brilliant! That's just what Buzz Aldrin did on the Apollo 11 mission! He made a switch out of a pen, too.

"What do you ink?" Alan jokes. "Should we go?"

Smiling, you use your pen-switch to turn on the engine. The rocket fires, and you and Alan jostle against each other as the ascent stage separates from the lower part of the lunar module, which will remain on the moon's surface. Down below, the moon buggy has cameras that watch the LM taking off for lunar orbit to dock with the CSM—and return to Earth.

Turn to page 172.

21

You don't panic. Why? You know there's never been a space mission where plans didn't change. As warning lights continue to flash all around you, you calmly ask, "Systems, can you give me an update?"

The answer comes immediately from a flight controller: "The space-craft guidance system has lost its attitude reference."

Uh-oh. A rocket with a bad attitude?
Maybe you **should** panic after all.
Draw a sulky, angry rocket here.
When you're done, turn to page 25.

The rocket's engines are way too powerful for such a light load! It's like building the *Titanic* to float a flea. You blast off much too quickly and over-shoot the moon.

Neptune, here you come!

## END

Like the idea of trying again?
Good, I **planet** that way!
Turn back to page 19.

Did you draw a pterodactyl? Turn to page 17. Was a creature from Mars in your picture? Go to page 118.

23

Aces! You've earned your job and the most important chair in the room. You feel a little bit like the king of space, don't you?

Draw yourself here as royalty. Why not give yourself a space crown and a star scepter? Be sure to include either a royal Martian or a pterodactyl. (Every space king should have one!)

FLIGHT DIRECTOR

When you're done, fold over the corner flap.

*Oh, I get it now! My apologies.*
*The flight controller said **altitude** . . . not **attitude**.*

The guidance system can't determine how high the rocket is—and it's still climbing, speeding toward space. You must get control back, but time is running out.

You remember what the flight director of Apollo 12 did. Your brother needs to reboot the computer on the rocket. And he needs to do it fast!

*Choose just the right words to give your brother the message.*
*There's no time for even a single wasted syllable!*

*As you travel from START to FINISH, what words are on your path?*

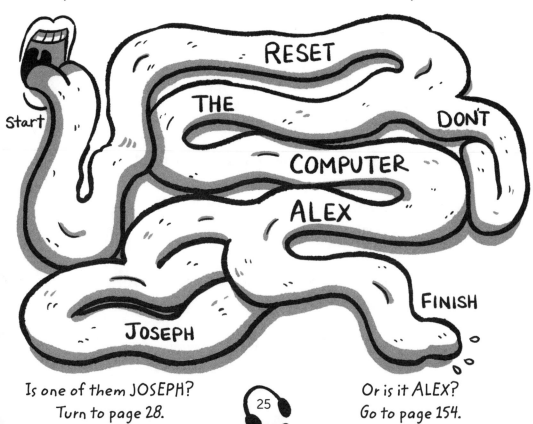

Start

RESET

THE

DON'T

COMPUTER

ALEX

FINISH

JOSEPH

Is one of them JOSEPH?
Turn to page 28.

25

Or is it ALEX?
Go to page 154.

"Thanks! At least the idea of being a sardine made me laugh!" your brother says over the radio. "Now let's get to the moon!"

"Twelve seconds till liftoff," Chuck announces.

"Start the ignition sequence!" you order.

A flight controller presses a button, and at T-minus 8.9 seconds—1,000 miles away—the rocket engines ignite! Flames blast from the most powerful rocket that has ever been built.

The rocket struggles to leave the ground, but strong clamps hold it in place—for now—as it builds up power. It's up to you to release the rocket at just the right time.

*As Chuck continues the countdown to liftoff,
construct your own launch platform.*

**"Five . . ."** *Draw finishing touches on the rocket.*

**"Four . . ."** *Tear along the line labeled A.*

**"Three . . ."** *Tear along the line labeled B.*

**"Two . . ."** *Fold up the two flaps along the line labeled C.*

**"One . . ."** *Draw flames coming out of the bottom of
the rocket.*

**"Zero!"** *Release the clamps! Pull the flap with the
clamps toward you to free the rocket!*

*Look at the back of that flap.
Follow the instructions you find there!*

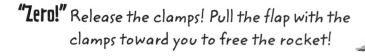

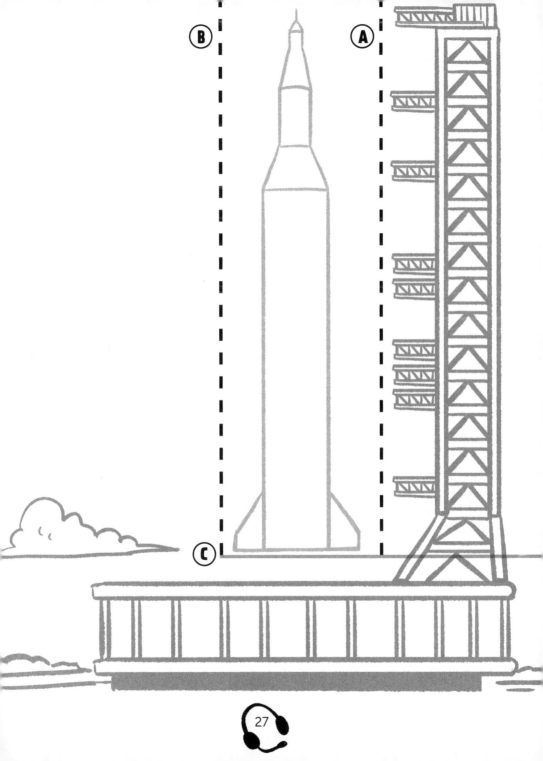

Turn to page 19.

BLASTOFF!

Two hundred miles away, a zookeeper hands Joseph the armadillo a message from you. Joseph looks at the message for a moment and then promptly . . .

. . . eats it.

Um, that's my way of telling you that no one named Joseph is on the current mission.

# END

Oh brother! Let's try that again! Go back to page 25.

Well done! The rocket carrying your brother, along with Buzz and Neil, lifts up into the sky. Thirty-six seconds into the flight, you're about to sigh with relief when—

*Craaack!* A flash fills the big screen at the front of the room. You see it strike the rocket.

"What was that?" you ask Chuck. "Was that lightning?"

*Craaack!* Another bolt from the sky hits the rocket.

Next to you, Chuck looks pale and worried. "The lightning has done something to the rocket's computer," he explains. "We can't tell how high the rocket is anymore!"

PAGE
179

*Um, that doesn't sound good. What do you do?*

*If you decide to cancel the mission, turn to page 31.*
*Want to keep going? Flip to page 22.*

After Alex uses the CSM's thrusters to move away from the lunar module, he swings the CSM around 180 degrees so it'll be ready to dock with the LM. He wants the probe on top of the CM to go into something called the drogue on top of the LM.

That's all a long way of saying: Help Alex get into position for docking!

1. Start in the space with the CSM in it.
2. Move right two spaces.
3. Travel up three spaces.
4. Go left one space.

5. Move down one space.
6. In the blank space at the bottom of the page, write the number you ended on.

| 36 | 38 | 36 | 38 | 36 |
|----|----|----|----|----|
| 38 | 36 | 38 | 36 | 38 |
| 36 | 38 | 36 | 38 | 36 |
| 38 | 36 | 38 | 36 | 38 |
|  | 38 | 36 | 38 | 36 |

Turn to page _____.

There are only two ABORT buttons in Mission Control. And you have one of them on your panel, under a little glass box. You hoped never to touch the button—because if you do, it means that something awful has happened and the mission must end.

What do you want to do?

Do you open the glass box so you can press the button? Fold over this flap.

Or do you change your mind and go back to page 29?

If you press this button,
the ABORT REQUEST
light will blink inside the
spacecraft and your brother
will pull the abort handle
immediately. He'll trust that
you've made the right call.

Are you really, really sure
you want to press that button?

Yes? Turn the page.
No? Go to page 22.

*Ka-BLAM!*

The launch escape system—a small rocket attached to the top of the astronauts' capsule—fires. The force of its blast jerks the command module off the top of the rocket. The capsule is tossed to the side, and it will make a safe landing in the water.

But your mission is over!

## END

I'm sure the astronauts are okay—but let's try another way! Go back to page 29.

You manage to get outside the service module to look at the site of the explosion. There's nothing you can do about the damage because you don't have the right tools to fix it. You head back inside the ship—

Or you *try* to. Sorry to say, your space suit from the 1960s reacts badly to space. The lack of air has turned the space suit so stiff and bulky that you can't fit through the hatch. Well, at least you have a great view from out here!

PAGE
180

# END

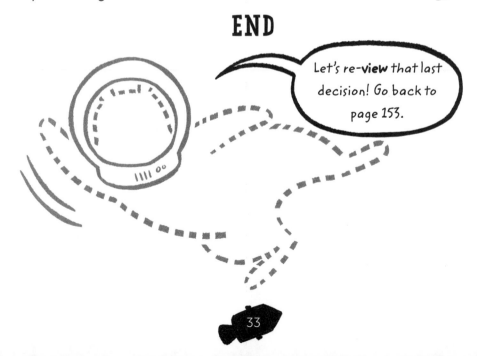

Let's re-**view** that last decision! Go back to page 153.

# Apollo Mission: A Most Puzzling Journey to the Moon

**EARTH**

START

FINISH

**1**

## See You Soon, Earth!

The Saturn V's rockets fire for about 12 minutes, putting the spacecraft into Earth orbit and then nudging it toward the moon.

**2**

**8**

### Y

## The Heat Is On!

Friction turns the CM into a flaming meteor as it reenters Earth's atmosphere. Three parachutes open, and the CM lands in the ocean.

### H

## Are We There Yet?

Apollo travels to reach moon orbit in about three days.

### T

## Bye, SM!

The SM is abandoned. Now only the CM is left, and it spins so its heat shields face Earth.

START at step 1 and then continue your journey! Match each blank puzzle piece on the map with its twin shape below. Then write the letter at the top of each shape in order in the blank spaces below.

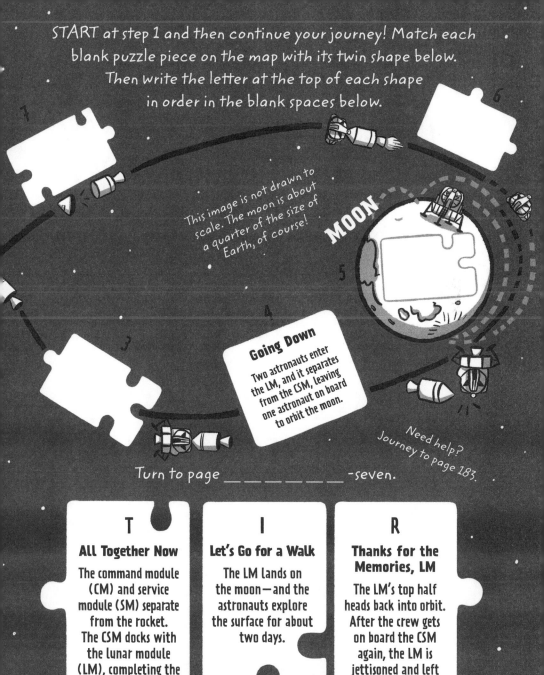

This image is not drawn to scale. The moon is about a quarter of the size of Earth, of course!

MOON

**Going Down**

Two astronauts enter the LM, and it separates from the CSM, leaving one astronaut on board to orbit the moon.

Need help? Journey to page 183.

Turn to page _____ -seven.

**T**

**All Together Now**

The command module (CM) and service module (SM) separate from the rocket. The CSM docks with the lunar module (LM), completing the Apollo spacecraft.

**I**

**Let's Go for a Walk**

The LM lands on the moon—and the astronauts explore the surface for about two days.

**R**

**Thanks for the Memories, LM**

The LM's top half heads back into orbit. After the crew gets on board the CSM again, the LM is jettisoned and left in space.

Congratulations! You helped Alex dock successfully with the spacecraft!
Too bad it's the *wrong* spacecraft.

# END

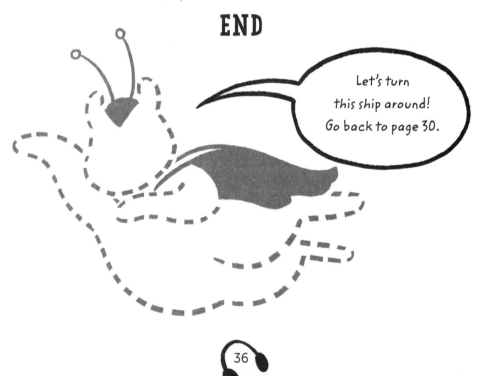

Let's turn
this ship around!
Go back to page 30.

"Boss!" Chuck's shout snaps you out of your thoughts. "We're ready for the CSM to separate and capture the lunar module."

*Uh, what on the moon does that mean? Oh yes, that was step two in the journey you were just reading about. Here's a refresher.*

The lunar module (LM) and command service module (CSM) are stacked on top of each other, but they're not in a ready-to-land-on-the-moon position. You need to rearrange the way they're stacked.

"Press the separation button, Alex," you tell your brother.

"We have detonation," Alex says a moment later. With a small explosion, the spacecraft splits apart as the CSM separates from the rest of the Saturn rocket. As the CSM pulls away, four panels on the end of the rocket open up. Now the lunar module (LM) is exposed.

*Draw the flames from the detonation here. When you're done, tear along the dotted lines and fold the flap over.*

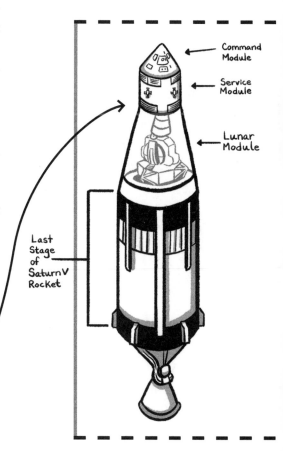

Command Module

Service Module

Lunar Module

Last Stage of Saturn V Rocket

Your brother trained for this docking a hundred times in the simulator on Earth. It should be as easy as breathing.

But something goes wrong. BOING! The CSM bounces off the LM when Alex attempts to dock. He tries again. And again. Each time your brother tries to dock, the two spacecraft bounce off each other.

"Give it a little more speed this time," you say.

Alex backs up the CSM and then rockets toward the LM much faster. "I feel like I'm going to crash into it!" he warns.

He does. Luckily, he doesn't do any real damage as the CSM bounces off again. The very end tip—or probe—of the CM won't stay inside the cone-shaped end—or drogue—of the LM.

*Turn to page 30.*

PAGE 177

*This reminds me of the time I was wearing my turbo wings and crashed into the window of the local Cineplex. To see what I mean, draw yourself smooshed up against this glass wall.* *Then turn to page 40.*

38

Once you're outside, you gaze up at the sky and wait for Sputnik to fly overhead.

Oh, there it is! Unfortunately, no one inside Mission Control knows where you've been for twenty minutes—and Chuck finally decided to cancel the mission!

So . . . hello, Sputnik! Goodbye, mission success!

# END

No problem—let's **go-pher** a do-over! Return to page 88.

If your brother can't dock with the LM, the moon landing will have to be canceled.

Alex says, "I don't . . . know . . . what to—" Suddenly he starts coughing uncontrollably for a few seconds. Finally, he stops and blurts, "Sorry about that!"

Then you hear Neil and Buzz start coughing, too. What's happening up there?

All you can think about is measles—an illness that's been going around here on Earth. Did Alex and the others catch it before they left? Are they about to get very sick in space?

Which problem should you tackle first?
The astronauts zinging through space at 24,000 miles per hour are depending on you to you keep them safe. This is a big decision!

Deal with the coughing?
Go to page 42.

Handle the docking problem?
Head to the simulator to get help
from Lynette on page 13.

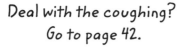

So you think it's the glove that's causing them to cough? Well, after you ask them to throw their gloves off the ship, you can wave goodbye to the mission!

# END

I'd **glove** to give you another chance! Go back to page 47.

"Doctor, how are Alex's vital signs?" you ask.

"He's not showing any signs of measles or flu," the flight surgeon responds. "Neither is Buzz or Neil."

"Can it just be motion sickness?" Alex gasps between coughing fits.

The flight surgeon shakes his head. "About half a gallon of liquid shifts toward your head when you're in space because gravity's not pulling the fluid to your legs anymore" he says. "That can make you feel sick, but it doesn't explain the coughing."

*Hmm. I'm having a tough time imagining how you could fit a half gallon of water in your head! Draw how this balloon head would look if you pumped that amount of liquid into it.* *When you're done, turn to page 88.*

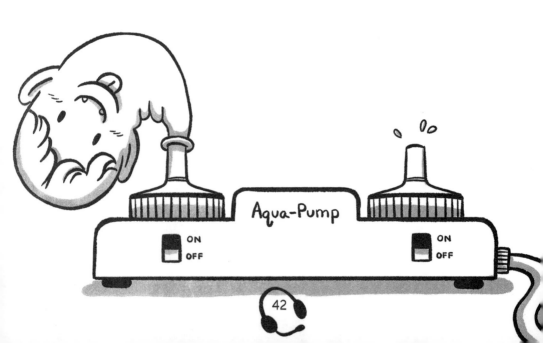

"Look at the wilting plant!" you say over your headset. "The underwear material must be making the astronauts cough!"

Lynette nods. "Ask the astronauts to seal their underwear in plastic bags, and all should be good."

You instruct Chuck to let the crew know their undies have to go in bags.

*You can just imagine how Alex will joke about that!*

You fixed the coughing problem!

*Do you still need to fix the docking problem?*
*Turn to page 13.*

*Do you still need to fix the docking problem?*
*Turn to page 13.*

*Already fixed it?*
*Head to page 54.*

"I'll keep you posted on our fuel level, but you'd better steer," Alan says. "I'm not feeling so great."

That's pretty obvious from his increasingly green face. You take the controls.

Somehow you have to make the fuel in the tank last until you can land. You need to *streeeetch* it out.

Think about the last time you ate pizza and the cheese
stretched from your hand to your mouth.
Draw that here!

When you're done,
turn to page 90.

So that's your choice? You think it's the food? Maybe it's the turkey dinner's revenge.

Um, that would be a solid *no*.

# END

I cry **fowl**! Trot to page 47 and try again.

The building where Lynette works is the size of an airplane hangar, and at its center is the enormous simulation chamber. All the air can be sucked out of the chamber to make it more like the vacuum of space.

Through the thick glass window, you can see Lynette inside the chamber. She's wearing her space suit and has three plants on a table in front of her.

"Lynette!" You bang on the window and then wave. "I need your help!" She can't hear you, of course, but she must have seen your arm moving.

Go to the next page.

Lynette turns on her radio headset. "Don't open that door!" she shouts. "I'm working to figure out why Alex, Neil, and Buzz are coughing. I have a theory that it's an object on board the spacecraft with them."

You'd better help your sister!

*Draw the specified items in the boxes. When you're done, tear along the dotted line and fold the flap up.*

PAGE 179

| a glove for a space suit | underwear | a turkey space meal |
| --- | --- | --- |
| | | |

The docking problem has you stumped, doesn't it? You decide to walk around the simulator, as if you might spot the answer you need. And guess what? You do.

A woman wearing glasses is leaning over a table, studying photographs of the docking mechanism.

That's Katherine Johnson! She's one of the "human computers" NASA hired to make incredible calculations to help with the mission.

PAGE
181

Katherine waves you over. "I've gone through all the numbers and calculations, and Alex is doing all the right things."

"So why can't he dock?" you ask.

"There must be something wrong with the latches of the docking mechanism," Katherine answers. "A tiny bit of dirt is probably blocking the latches from closing. The crew just needs to manually open and close the latches. That might shake the dirt loose."

Go to the next page.

What's causing the trouble on the spacecraft?
Turn to the page number for the item you identify as the source.

45

43

41

You rush back to the control room and ask the crew to give Katherine's idea a try.

Hoping to shake loose any dirt particles, Neil and Buzz lock and unlock the latches. And then Alex maneuvers the CSM around for one more try at docking with the LM.

*To see whether the plan works, fold up the page corner and connect the probe and the drogue. But do not tear the page! Which drogue can you connect with?*

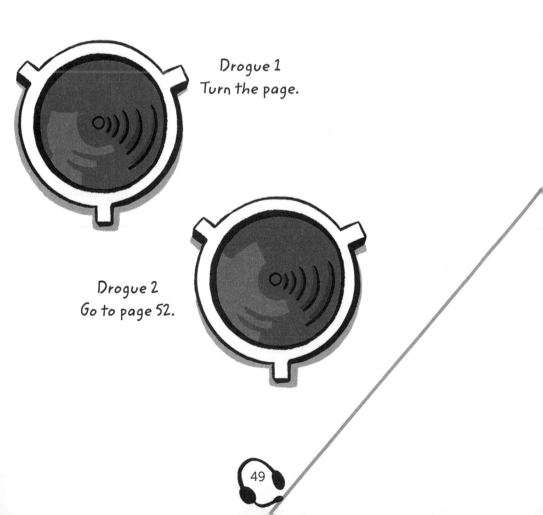

Drogue 1
Turn the page.

Drogue 2
Go to page 52.

I definitely just heard something, and it sounded like this: *Snap!*

Here's a hint for the next time you're docking with a vehicle in space: Don't come in at the wrong angle, or you'll break the probe off your command module.

Mission Control is aborting the mission!

# END

Let's **go-pher** a different ending. It'll be *a snap!* Go back to page 49.

"Okay, Houston, we've had a problem here," you say through your radio. *Hmm, that sounds very familiar.*

PAGE 177

Mission Control responds instantly. "Are you three okay?"

"Roger that," you answer, but actually you're not sure.

After all, part of the spacecraft has just blown off! And you're tens of thousands of miles away from Earth. There is no rest stop or gas station where you can pull over to ask for help.

*Though, what if there were?*
*Draw a floating gas station with a service garage here.*

When you're done,
go to page 153.

Success! After the CSM and LM click together, they're connected by a hatchway.

"Thank you!" Alex tells you. "And please thank Katherine for us. Who knew she was a mathematician *and* a mechanic?"

You think about the perfect thank-you gift to give Katherine.
Draw it here.
Then if you still need to fix the coughing problem, go to page 42. If not, head to page 54.

Yes! That's right! You pop the slide back into the pneumatic tube and send it across the room to the systems controller, who will put it up on the big screen for you to see even better.

Now it's clear how truly incomplete the map is! You feel doubt creep in. If you make a mistake . . . your brother and his crewmate might not make it back to the CM.

As Alex describes to you the boulders and craters he can see on the surface, you feel a hand touch your shoulder. It's Lynette. She gives you a smile. "You can do this."

*I hope she's right. Turn to page 56 to find out.*

The next few hours are a blur as the astronauts prepare for the upcoming stage of the mission—landing on the moon!

Your brother and Neil Armstrong climb into the lunar module and detach from the command module.

As the lunar module plummets toward the surface of the moon, alarms blare, and a number starts blinking on the big screen in Mission Control.

1202  1202  1202  1202  1202  1202
1202  1202
1202  1202  1202  1202  1202
1202  1202  1202  1202  1202

"Chuck, what does that number mean?" you ask.

Chuck shakes his head. "I don't know what that code is, boss. But the computer guiding the LM is failing."

You look around the room. Codes and their meanings have been taped up and displayed along one wall. Can you find the one you're looking for? You're running out of time!

54

Go to the next page.

A → ← A

Oh, I suppose I can help you focus
on what you need to see. Fold this
page so that the As touch at the
top and the Bs at the bottom.

Based on what you find,
what do you say next?

"Let's keep going!" Turn to page 58.
"Abort the mission!" Go to page 147.

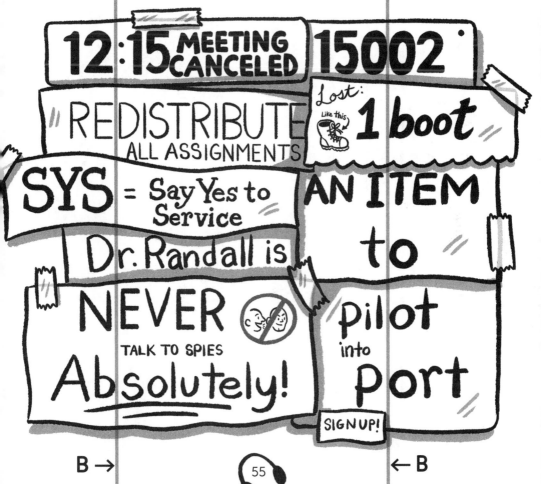

Can you help Alex bring the lunar module safely to the surface?
Follow your instincts.

**Step 1:** Finish the map on the big screen by filling in the two boulders you saw on the slide.

**Step 2:** Lift up the screen on page 57 so that your writing hand can duck behind it and write on page 59. No peeking!

**Step 3:** Using the main map on the screen as a guide, draw the path from Start that Alex will need to take to land the lunar module safely. I'm trusting you not to look!

**Step 4:** Once you think you're in the safe landing zone, draw an X and check to make sure.

**Step 5:** If you pass over or landed in a deep crater, on a slope, or on a boulder . . . try again until you bring the LM down in the Safe Landing Zone. When you do, turn to page 67.

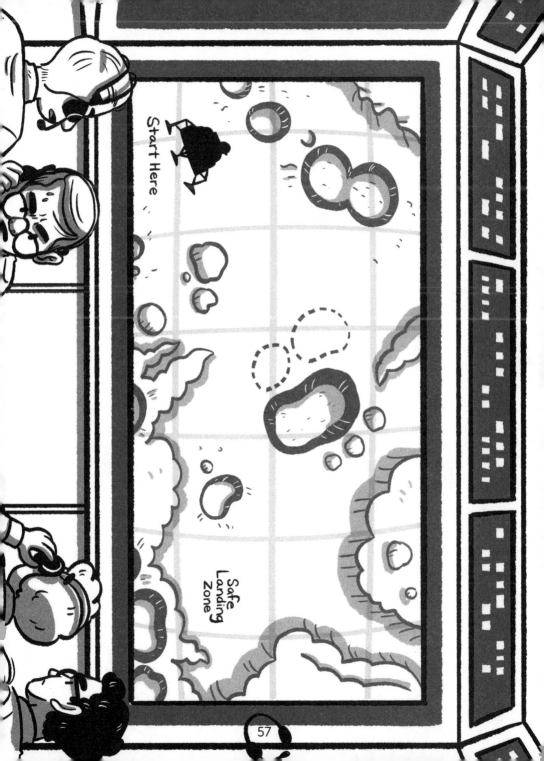

You explain to Chuck what you've found. And he calms down a little, too.

"Now I remember!" he shouts. "The code 1202 means too much data is coming in at once. The LM's computer can't handle all that information. The only way to fix it is to restart it."

PAGE **176**

There's no time to reboot the computer. The LM is falling too fast toward the surface!

*You feel as nervous as a giraffe on banana peels in a china shop. Draw that scene here. When you're done, turn to page 61.*

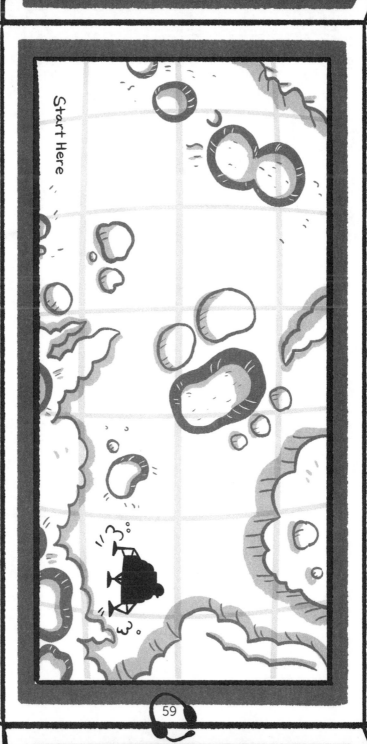

Start Here

You use the photo you picked to give Alex directions. He follows them perfectly and lands smoothly on . . .

. . . my aunt Edna's front lawn.

Yes, that's right. You chose the wrong slide.

# END

Let's try for a **picture**-perfect ending! Return to page 64.

"No one has been able to land the lunar module in the simulator without the computer," Alex says quickly. "The LM's thrusters are way too tricky to control without help!"

"Stay calm, Alex," you tell your brother, even though your own heart is pounding. "I'll give you directions. Just do what I tell you!"

To bring the LM down for a safe landing, you need just the right map of the moon. You know it's in one of the staff support rooms way down the hall and on a different floor. A collection of photographs of maps is kept there.

But you don't have time to call on the phone and explain what you want. The technicians in that room need to *see* what you're thinking.

PAGE
176

You can't send an email or a text. Those kinds of communication don't exist yet. But there is the pneumatic tube (p-tube) system!

Pressurized air shoots 12-inch by 3-inch aluminum canisters with paper messages through sealed pipes from one p-tube station to another. Messages can be delivered around the building within tens of seconds.

61

Turn to page 63 to use the p-tubes!

You look more closely at the photo and know instantly that you picked the wrong one.

It's actually a zoomed-in picture of my last birthday party. You can't tell, but Amicus has baked my favorite cake—persimmon deluxe.

# END

Let's cook up a better ending.
Go back to page 64.

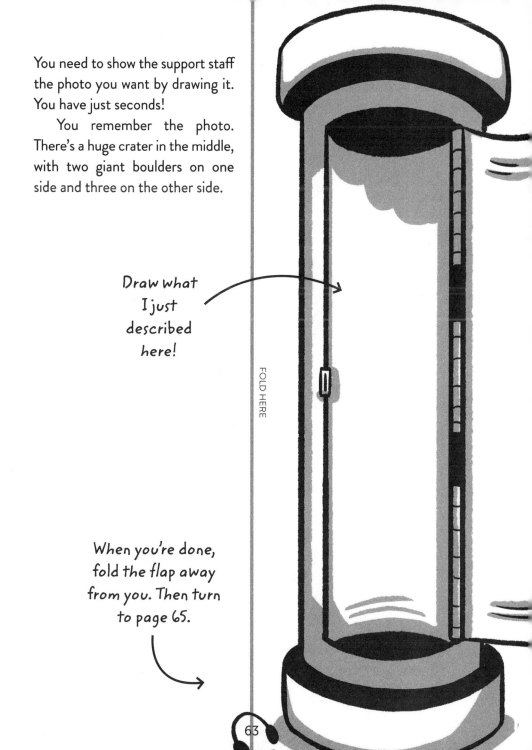

You need to show the support staff the photo you want by drawing it. You have just seconds!

You remember the photo. There's a huge crater in the middle, with two giant boulders on one side and three on the other side.

Draw what I just described here!

When you're done, fold the flap away from you. Then turn to page 65.

FOLD HERE

*Dear Flight Director,*

*These three slides with photographs of maps of the moon are the closest to your drawing. Which one did you have in mind?*

*—Vehicle Systems*

Which slide looks most like the drawing you made?
Quick! Choose one!

#1

#2

#3

Slide #1: Go to page 53.
Slide #2: Flip to page 60.
Slide #3: Head to page 62.

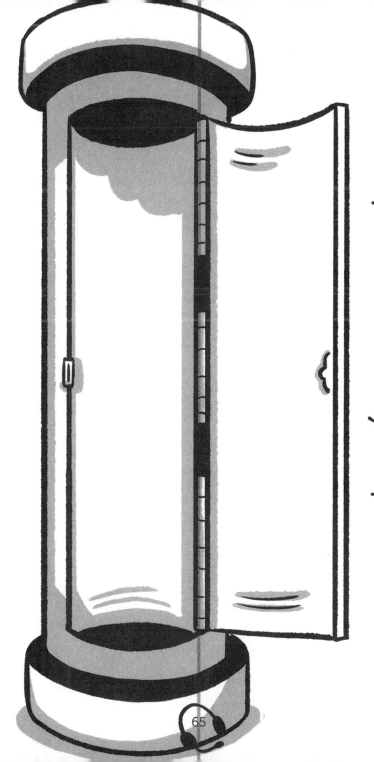

Fold this flap over to close your pneumatic tube!

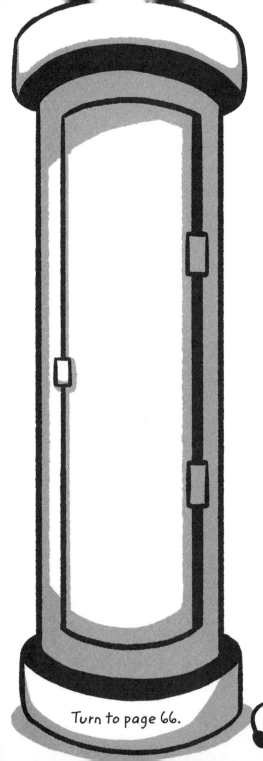

You drop the canister into the hatch in the console in front of you. With a *ker-pfft!* of air, it shoots off into the p-tube system.

You have to wait for the support staff to send their response back to you . . . and the seconds seem like years. Your brother and Neil need you—they have no idea where to land, and the engine for landing is just about out of fuel!

1202 1202
1202 1202
1202 1202
1202 1202
1202

*Pffft!*
The p-tube canister has come back! To open it, turn to page 64 and unfold the flap to see what's inside the p-tube.

Turn to page 66.

For a moment, no one in Mission Control moves. And the astronauts are quiet, too.

What just took place must have been so gentle that the crew didn't even feel it.

But thanks to the lights on your control panel, you know that something major has occurred.

You want Alex to realize it on his own. And he does.

A loud sound travels from the moon, across hundreds of thousands of miles of space, up through your panel, and into your headset. It's a shout of joy coming from Alex.

A second later, he says, "Houston, we've landed."

Jumping up and down, you and Lynette hug as the Mission Control center bursts into cheers!

Turn to page 172.

# MOON BUGGY DRIVER PATH

Welcome to the ultimate driving test!

I'm not convinced you're ready to drive on the moon.
Prove me wrong! Steer each of these three vehicles by following
the instructions for holding your pen or pencil. Try drawing a
line from START to FINISH without running into anything.
If you hit an obstacle, you have to start over!

**START**

### EASY
Hold your pen or pencil
with two fingers
and your thumb.

68

When you can drive all three vehicles
without crashing, turn to page 71.

**FINISH**

**MEDIUM**
Hold your pen or pencil with
one finger and your thumb.

**SUPER TRICKY**
Use any two fingers to
hold your pen or pencil—
**except** your thumb.

69

"We're landing RIGHT NOW!" you shout.

"Wait—" Alan starts to say, but you're not listening. You're too busy bringing the lunar module down as fast as you can.

When you slam into the moon's surface, snapping off two of the LM's legs, you wonder, "Did I land too soon and too fast?"

*Do I really need to answer that?*

# END

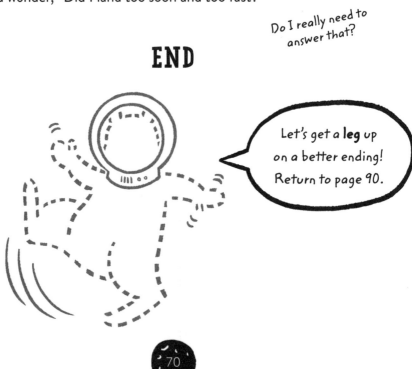

Let's get a **leg** up on a better ending! Return to page 90.

Hmm. You could still use training. But there's no time!

Right now, you and your two crewmates—Jim Lovell and Alan Shepard—are orbiting the moon in the incredibly cramped capsule called the command module, or CM. This capsule has been your home since you blasted off from Earth three days ago and made your way to the moon.

There's one thing the CM can't do—land on the moon. So Jim will stay up in orbit in the CM, and you and Alan will head down to the surface in the lunar module (LM).

Alan is already in the LM. Join him by tearing along the dotted lines and folding the flap away from you, like this:

After you fold the flap, turn the page.

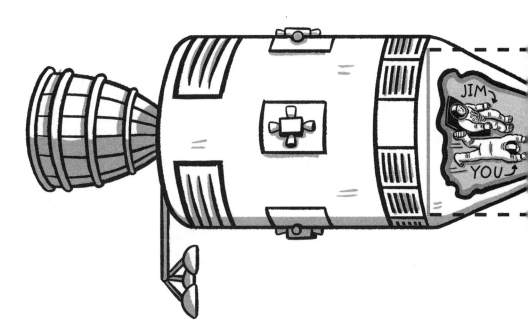

"Hey! Hey!" Alan calls from about five inches away when you board the lunar module. "I don't know if you can see me in all this space! Here I am!"

You laugh. The tiny LM is just 160 cubic feet—that's the size of a large closet—and it's made to house two astronauts for up to three days while they're on the moon.

*The LM's walls are almost as thin as aluminum foil.*
*That's not much different from the thickness of this page.*
*To see what I mean, use a pen or pencil to poke a hole*
*here and here in the walls of the LM. Then turn to page 85.*

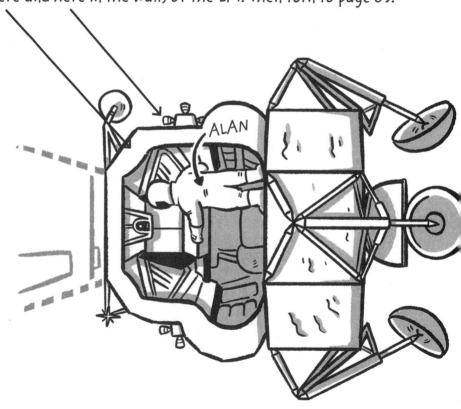

ALAN

"Be good while we're gone, Jim! Don't throw any parties!" Alan jokes as he closes the hatch between the CM and the LM.

    With the hatch shut, you and Alan are alone in LM. You turn to get a better look at the cockpit.

    Um. Wow. If what you see doesn't make you nervous, what I'm going to say should: This. Path. Is. About. To. Get. Very. Tricky.

Ready to separate from the CM and descend to the moon's surface? First, draw the missing buttons and levers. Be sure to include their numbers. Now connect them in order. In the blank below, write the shape you made. Then follow the directions.

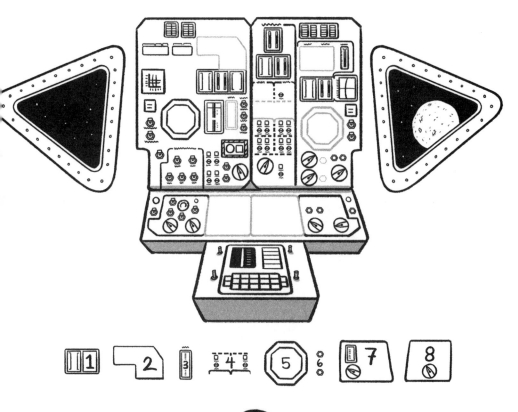

Need help?
Go to page 183.

Turn to page 7 _____ .

You lower your ship into the crater and wait for the impact of landing on the surface.

And wait . . .

And wait . . .

No one has ever explored this crater, and it seems to go on forever!

You're still falling when you run out of fuel!

# END

Don't worry! I see a light at the end of the tunnel. Follow it to return to page 87!

Aces!

The good news: You've undocked from the CM, and you have 12 whole minutes to pilot the LM down to the moon.

The bad news: You're plummeting toward the lunar surface at thousands of miles per hour from a height of 50,000 feet.

Draw something to slow your fall—
a parachute, wings, or a heavy rocket.

When you're done, fold over this flap.

75

Smile for the camera! About 600 million people have tuned in to watch this moment on their black-and-white televisions. That's one-fifth of the population on Earth watching you take your first step on another world!

You told your family you would draw a special picture for them in the lunar regolith—the moon's soft, sandy surface. Make it a good one! The lack of any wind or atmosphere on the moon means your drawing will stay there forever.

Unless I don't like it—I might rocket up there to erase it.

If you drew
a parachute or wings,
turn to page 113.

Did you draw a heavy rocket?
Go to page 79.

Did you draw yourself into the picture?

Yes—turn to page 78.
No—go to page 139.

I would say that's an amazing decision!

I would, that is, if I really felt that way.

While it would taste delicious with some tomato sauce, a brittle piece of pasta is not going to help you with the broken switch. But you'll have plenty of time to mull that over as you sit inside the lunar lander . . . for a very, very long time.

# END

SNAP!

Who says you can't change the **past**-a? Snap back to page 117.

Alan climbs down to the surface behind you and stumbles.

"Are you okay?" you ask over your radio headset.

"I'm fine—" Alan starts to answer, but he's interrupted by Mission Control.

"No, you're not, Alan. We can see your vitals, and your breathing and heart rate are too high. After you help plant the flag, please go back into the LM and rest."

Alan nods. His face shows his disappointment, but he understands. "Roger that, Mission Control."

Oh, even I feel sorry for Alan. To come all the way to the moon and have to stay behind in the LM? That's hard! Fill in the flag you plant in the moon's surface— and give it an amazing design to help cheer up Alan.

78

When you're done, turn to page 89.

Brilliant choice! A heavy descent rocket is the only way to control how quickly you land. But if you use it wrong, you could flip over when you reach the surface.

Oh! Did I mention there's only enough fuel for one landing attempt? In other words, you have to get this right the first time.

See the lunar surface below? Make sure the LM is descending at the correct angle. Tear along the dotted lines and fold over the flap of the engine blast that will help you land level on the slanted surface.

A

B

# SNAP!

Remember how you once made a rubber band stretch farther than anyone else in your class could? All your friends' bands snapped, but yours kept *streeeetching....*

You think you can do the same thing here with the tank of fuel.

But, sadly, I'm afraid you're wrong. The fuel ran out a few seconds ago. You are now plunging out of control toward the surface, which you'll hit with a—

*SNNNNAAAP!*

**END**

SNAP

Let's return to page 90 and try again. This time it'll be a **snap!**

Flip to page 83.

Go to page 105.

BLASTOFF!

"Woo-hoo!" Fred shouts as if he's on the best roller-coaster ride of his life.

And you feel the same way. What a heart-pounding thrill!

The rocket burns 15 tons of fuel every second as it pushes you toward the sky. Just to get out of Earth's atmosphere, you'll burn almost a million gallons of fuel!

It's like you're riding a tornado—maybe a few of them!

*Draw three tornadoes under the rocket and then turn to page 140.*

You can't wait to show the folks at NASA what you've collected on the moon. They'll be so surprised!

And I think you will be, too, when you realize what's actually in your bag. . . .

# END

Let's rock and roll to page 109 to try again!

Well, call me impressed. You might actually have the right stuff. . . .

Oh, wait, the computer is trying to tell you something. It's an alarm. And I don't think it's good.

**1202 . . . 1202 . . .**

"Mission Control?" Alan speaks into the radio in his space suit, calling back to Earth. "Do you see this down there? What's a 1202 alarm?"

"Uh, give us a second," Mission Control answers. For the first time you can remember, Mission Control sounds worried. "We'll figure it out. In the meantime, go ahead and turn off the alarm."

I know! I know what it is! The same thing happened on the Apollo 11 mission.

PAGE
**176**

To switch off the alarm, tear along
the dotted lines and fold over the two
flaps with **1202** flashing on them.
Continue folding over the adjacent (next)
flaps until you get to blank screens.
How many times in total did you see the
word **ALARM** on the back of the two flaps?
Write that number in the blank.

Go to page 8 _____.

Need help?
Flip to page 183.

83

1202 1202

1202 1202

1202 1202

1202 1202

1202

84

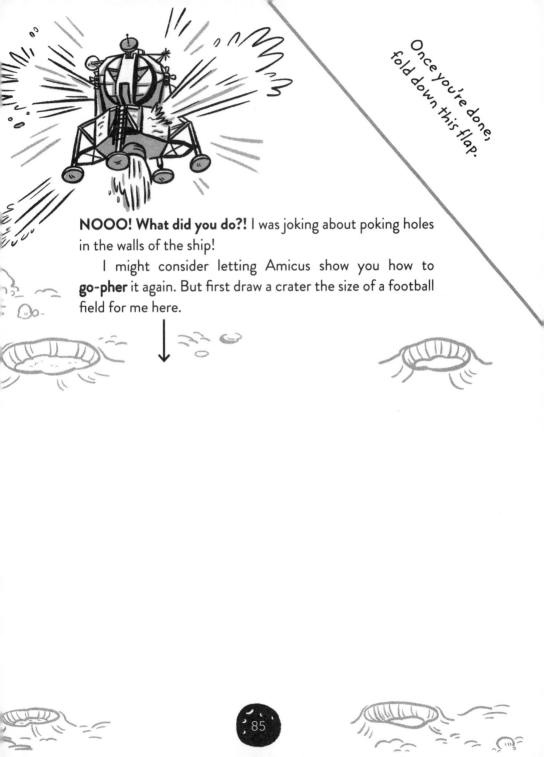

Once you're done, fold down this flap.

**NOOO! What did you do?!** I was joking about poking holes in the walls of the ship!

I might consider letting Amicus show you how to **go-pher** it again. But first draw a crater the size of a football field for me here.

"Let's make this a hole lot better. Keep moving to page 75."

"We're a go on the alarm," Mission Control says. A "go" means Mission Control wants the mission to continue.

Alan doesn't seem convinced. In fact, he looks downright green. "Are you sure, Mission Control?"

"Yes," Mission Control responds. "The computer that's controlling your speed and your orientation is overloaded. There's too much information. We need to restart it."

Rebooting your computer will take two minutes—a long time when you're falling to the surface of the moon with limited fuel.

Oh, and have you looked out the window lately? Tear along the dotted lines and fold over the flap to take a look.

*Go to the next page.*

That's right. You're heading for a crater that's the size of a football field. (Don't blame me! You're the one who drew it!)

Just like the crew of the Apollo 11 mission, you have only 90 seconds' worth of fuel left, a computer that's overloaded, and a mammoth crater dead ahead.

PAGE
180

"What should we do?" Alan asks you. *Good question, Alan.*

*If you decide to land in the crater, turn to page 74.*
*If you think you can make it to the other side,*
*turn to page 44.*

If the coughing problem isn't due to motion sickness, what could it be? You need some time to think.

"Keep an eye on things, Chuck," you say. "I'll be right back."

Chuck's eyes go wide. "Where are you going?"

*Good question. Where exactly are you going?*

If you rush to find Lynette, turn to page 46.

If you run outside to look for the satellite Sputnik for inspiration, turn to page 39.

Aces! Once the flag is in place, Alan climbs back up the LM's ladder. You promise to keep checking in by radio, and then you wave goodbye.

"Don't worry. I'll be fine! Now get out there and find those anorthosites for NASA!" Alan says before he disappears inside.

*Um, what on Earth—or in space—are anorthosites?*
*Monster ants? A walking website? Moon flowers?*

*Whatever you think anorthosites are, draw them here.*
*When you're done, turn to page 102.*

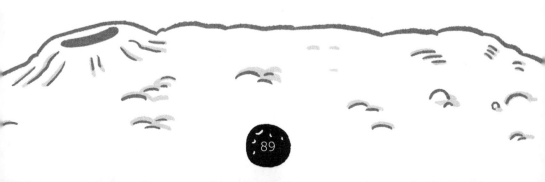

Aces! You made it over the crater, but you still need to land.

"Thirty seconds' worth of fuel left!" Alan says.

You must bring the lunar module down . . . or abandon the journey.

I see a flat area ahead! Actually, there are a few possibilities.

*Which spot will you try?*

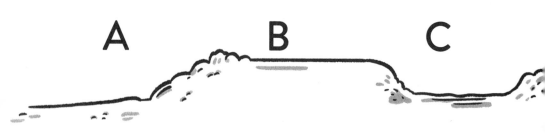

Fuel

A: Go to page 70.
B: Turn to page 162.
C: Flip to page 80.

It's time to drive the moon buggy! Instead of a steering wheel, you find a T-shaped controller for steering and changing speed. You might have a tough time getting the hang of it, so you'd better plan your route!

Keep in mind that NASA has a very strict rule: You can drive only as far as your oxygen supply would allow you to walk back if the buggy were to break down.

Your tank has enough air that you can walk from point A to point B.

A  B

Which path will you take?

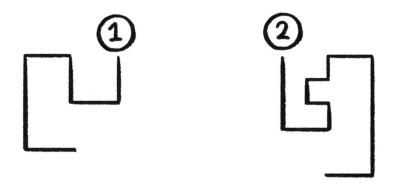

Did you choose to
drive path #1?
Go to page 108.

Did you choose to
drive path #2?
Flip to page 95.

*Yes! Excellent idea! You actually need to*
*go forward if you want to return to Earth.*

You had always planned on traveling around the moon . . . but that's more important than ever now. While you won't land on the lunar surface, the moon is going to save your lives.

"Prepare to perform a gravity assist around the moon," you tell Fred and Jack.

As you approach the moon, its gravity will grab your ship and pull you closer. You'll whip around the moon as it orbits Earth and gain even more speed. Then the moon will act like a slingshot and fling you back toward Earth with extra power. That will get you home faster . . . before you run out of oxygen!

You get a "gravity assist" every day when you go down a hill or ramp. To see what I mean, get the spacecar on page 93—it's out of fuel—to the finish line.

*Draw the correct ramps in the two blank circles so that the*
*spacecar will coast along to the finish. Use a ramp only once.*
*Write the numbers of the ramps you choose in order in*
*the blanks. Then follow the instructions.* *I've done the*
*first one for you.*
*Because I'm*
*amazing.*

Turn to page 1 ___ ___ .

*Need help?*
*Slingshot to page 183.*

92

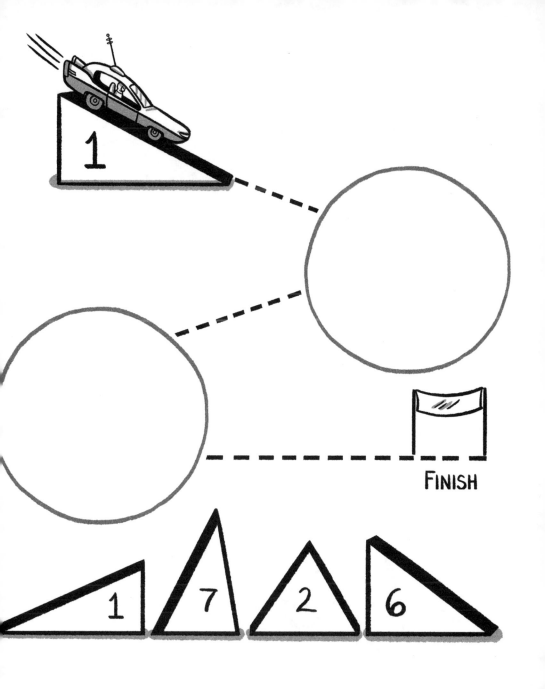

1

FINISH

1  7  2  6

"That's the contact light!" Alan shouts. "That means we've landed!"

"Then why do you look so upset?" you ask, confused by the expression on his face.

Alan points out the window. "I'm not sure exactly *where* we've landed!"

"Uh-oh," you mutter as you take a look, too.

You said it, my friend. Uh-oh indeed.

# END

That's a monster of an ending! Try again on page 162.

You can almost imagine the wind in your hair as you cruise happily across the surface of the moon. You only wish NASA had put a radio on board the buggy—that way you could blast your favorite tune.

That song wouldn't be "You've Gone Too Far from the LM," would it?

A good question to think about when the buggy breaks down and you're stuck in the middle of nowhere.

## END

Let's hitch a ride back to page 91 and try again!

Excellent! After all that work collecting old rocks, you deserve a snack! Luckily, your space suit has an in-suit drinking device, or canteen. You can drink water from one bag or sip food through a straw from the other bag. Yum! I love food in bags!

What do you want in your bag?

Draw your favorite meal here in the blender. Then give it a whirl! Now draw that meal pouring from the blender into a bag. Ugh! That looks DIS-gusting! Please turn to page 110 immediately.

You and Alan cheer! That blue light means the LM's feet have come in contact with the moon's surface. You've touched down so smoothly that neither of you felt anything!

"I don't know why you were so worried," Alan says with a laugh. "There's two seconds' worth of fuel remaining."

You shut down the engine, and it's suddenly quiet. Mission Control is waiting to hear what words you will speak next. And so am I.

You know they will go down in history as your first words spoken over the radio from the moon. I know what Neil Armstrong said . . . but what words will you choose?

PAGE **180**

### Quick! Write down examples of these words!

adjective: _____     adjective: _____

adjective: _____     adjective: _____

animal: _____     food item: _____

adverb: _____

---

When you're done,
tear along the dotted line
and fold over the flap.

"Well," Alan says, chuckling weakly at your words, "that was something."

Your crewmate is clearly sick, and not only because of what you just said. He's holding his stomach but manages a small smile. "Let's suit up and get outside!" he says.

A space suit is a like a portable spacecraft. It has everything you need to survive. But it can take a long time to put on!

You are already wearing your pressure suit. But to go for a moonwalk, you'll need to add . . .

- **protective overboots**

- **gloves with rubber fingertips**

- **filters/visors for your helmet to protect you from sunlight**

- **a portable life support backpack with oxygen and cooling water**

*Go to the next page.*

*Use the words you wrote to fill in the blanks.*
*I can't wait for people on Earth to hear what you have to say!*

"Mission Control, the _____ and
adjective

_____    _____
adjective                         animal

has_____ landed like a(n)
adverb

_____ and _____
adjective                              adjective
_____ ."
food item

*Turn the page.*

Together, the space suit and backpack weigh 180 pounds on Earth—but only 30 pounds on the moon, thanks to its low gravity!

*Draw each item onto your suit, and then turn the page.*

After you and Alan have helped each other get into your space suits, you open the hatch of the LM.

**Hatch**
You exit and enter the spacecraft through the hatch.

**Ladder**
You use the ladder to climb down to the lunar surface and back up into the spacecraft.

*Hold on! You're missing something important! Draw the ladder here so you can climb down to the moon's surface. Once you have the ladder in place, keep going!*

As your foot sinks into the soft, sandy surface, the enormity of the moment hits you: You are standing on another world. Over the horizon, you can see home . . . Earth. You did it!

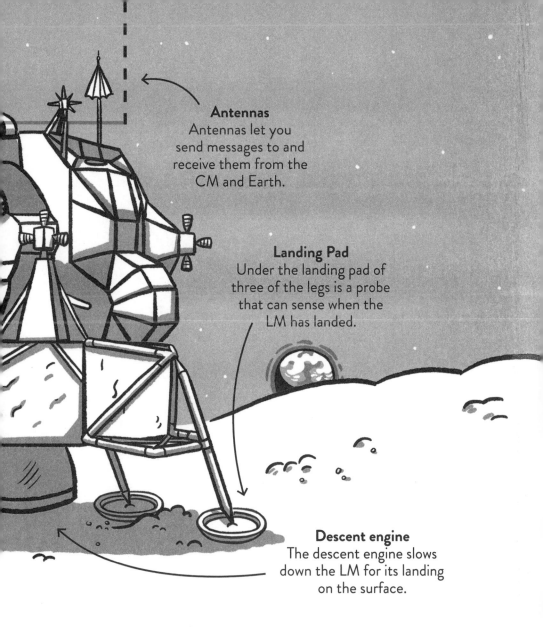

**Antennas**
Antennas let you
send messages to and
receive them from the
CM and Earth.

**Landing Pad**
Under the landing pad of
three of the legs is a probe
that can sense when the
LM has landed.

**Descent engine**
The descent engine slows
down the LM for its landing
on the surface.

Once you've taken a good look at the LM,
tear along the dotted lines, fold over the flap,
and follow the radio instructions from Earth.

Turn to page 76.

Ah! Anorthosites are the moon's oldest rocks! I actually knew that all along because I'm a genius!

As you know, you can jump super high on the moon thanks to its lower gravity. In fact, a basketball player could jump six times as high on the moon as on Earth. But walking around in a bulky space suit is exhausting, and you'll only get about 330 feet away from the LM before you get tired.

6 feet

5 feet

4 feet

3 feet

2 feet

1 foot

EARTH                    MOON

Go to the next page.

Luckily, the folks at NASA have been dreaming up different vehicles that astronauts can drive on the moon. Which one did they send on your mission?

*Starting at the top, draw what you think each vehicle looks like. Then tear along the dotted lines to fold over the flaps.*

# LUNAR WORM

# LUNAR LEAPER

# LUNAR ROVER

Turn to page 106.

You're coming in too fast sideways. As you bring the LM down for a landing, it tips over!

# END

Did you choose the wrong engine blast? Go back to page 79!

Say hello to your new ride!

The moon buggy is folded flat against the LM to make it easy to bring to the moon. Normally, it would take two astronauts to unpack it, but I suppose I can unfold it for you. After all, it cost $38 million—that's over $200 million in today's money—and I'd hate to see you scratch it.

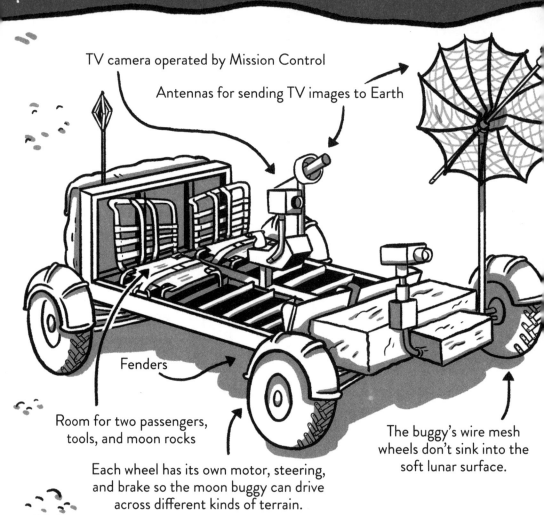

TV camera operated by Mission Control

Antennas for sending TV images to Earth

Fenders

Room for two passengers, tools, and moon rocks

Each wheel has its own motor, steering, and brake so the moon buggy can drive across different kinds of terrain.

The buggy's wire mesh wheels don't sink into the soft lunar surface.

Go to the next page.

The vehicle weighs about 460 pounds on Earth—
one-sixth the weight of a compact car—but can
carry more than twice its weight.

You know what this buggy is missing?
A license plate! Draw your own here.

When you're done, check out the
license plate I put on my carriage.
Use it to fill in the blank.

Turn to page _____.

9TIMES10PLUS1

Need help?
Flip to page 183.

Aces! At a speed of about eight miles per hour, you catch some air as you cruise over a small hill.

Yes, it's quite enjoyable to drive around in one's own buggy, but it's time to collect those anorthosites. And Mission Control wants you to collect 10 pounds of them from different parts of the moon.

When you find exactly 10 pounds, unscramble the letters on the rocks you found.

T
13 pounds

A
1.5 pounds

R
4 pounds

S
0.1 pounds

9 pounds

12 pounds

9.2 pounds

2.5 pounds

0.5 pounds

11 pounds

1.5 pounds

Do the letters spell **LUNAR**?
Turn to page 96.

Did you spell **ROVER**?
Go to page 82.

Alan is in trouble! Get back to the LM! You grab for the controller too quickly, and your gloved hand hits the panel behind it with a *crack!* Oh my.

Um, the computer you just destroyed kept track of the distance each wheel traveled. That way it could retrace your exact movement back to the LM inch by inch. But not anymore! And a normal Earth compass won't work up here—there's no magnetic field to turn the compass's needle.

So how will you find your way back to the LM? Everything on the lunar surface looks the same. Luckily, NASA trains each astronaut for just such an emergency—and you know how to read a sun compass.

The sun compass looks like this. ⟶

*Go to the next page.*

But I don't have time to give you a refresher course on how it works. So let's just use this stick I've put in the lunar surface for you.

Fold down this corner to bring the sun over the horizon and follow the shadow the stick would cast at that moment.

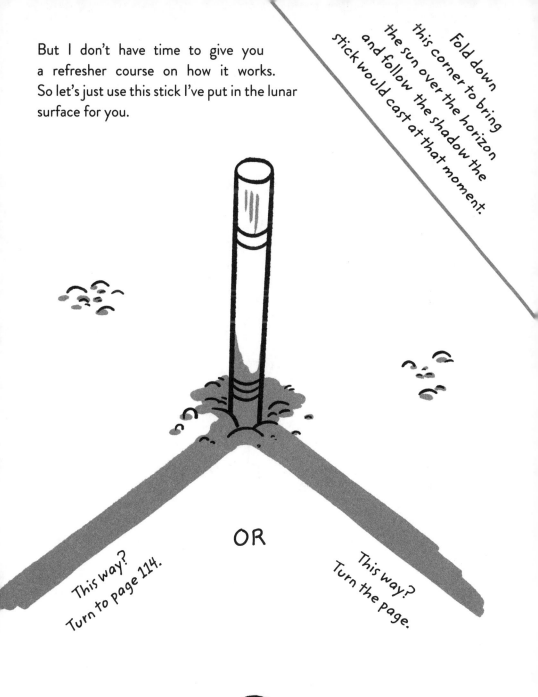

OR

This way? Turn to page 114.

This way? Turn the page.

You don't find the LM. But good news! You discover an amazing crater filled with incredible slopes—the perfect spot to practice your moon buggy jumps.

Bad news! Your buggy runs out of power mid-jump. Looks like the fun is over!

# END

Let's **leap** to a better ending. Bound back to page 111 and try again!

Ahh . . . very interesting choice. But the wrong one.

There is no atmosphere around the moon, so wings and parachutes have nothing to catch hold of. They are useless! Even in the low gravity, you fall like a rock to the surface of the moon—and, well . . .

Don't worry. We'll make it **well.** Go back to page 75.

Aces! I'm very impressed. But you still have one of the greatest challenges ahead of you. Now that you know the direction of the lunar module, you need to take a couple of shortcuts to get there!

It's very important your path goes from START to FINISH without backtracking! Write the letters on your path in order in the blanks, and then follow the directions.

Need help? Turn to page 183!

___ ___ ___ ___ ___   ___ ___   ___ ___ ___ ___   ___ ___ ___ .

**START**

FINISH

Okay! I think you're ready to go around the moon.

I need to warn you: As you complete this maneuver, the moon blocks all signals to Earth. That means the three of you won't be able to talk to Mission Control for a few minutes.

Only a handful of people have been so far from other humans and so alone.

*To get an idea of what I mean, draw a scene from a movie about what you and your two crewmates do to nervously pass the time during the radio silence.*

Go to page 165.

Quick! You must replace the broken switch. That's the only way to close the circuit and arm the engine.

PAGE 178

You glance around. . . . Alan hasn't touched his spaghetti lunch. Could you use spaghetti?

Unsure, you look down at your writing hand. Maybe you could use your pen?

*Whichever object you choose,*
*draw it in the place of the broken switch.*

Did you use a
long piece of pasta?
Go to page 77.

117

Did you draw
a pen or pencil?
Turn to page 20.

You settle into your throne next to your Martian—er, I mean, your chair next to a computer—and wave to Chuck, your second-in-command, who sits next to you. He keeps all the mission checklists in his head and knows exactly what's supposed to happen and when.

"Hey, boss," Chuck greets you with a grin, bouncing with excitement. "T-minus five minutes!"

*"T" stands for the time the rocket is scheduled to launch. So it's five minutes till blastoff! Better check in with the crew on board the rocket 1,000 miles away.*

"Apollo, this is Mission Control," you say through your headset. "Are you a go?"

"Absolutely!" your brother responds from the rocket. "All I know is go!"

You laugh. "How's it going in the command module, big brother?"

*Oh, right. I forgot to mention this: Your brother is an astronaut, and he's the flight commander of this Apollo mission!*

A fuzzy black-and-white image of your brother with Neil Armstrong and Buzz Aldrin flashes on the big screen at the front of the room.

*Go to the next page.*

"Well, we're sitting on top of thirty-six stories of highly explosive fuel," your brother answers with a chuckle, "and we're a little snug here in the command module."

*Maybe you can help your brother, Buzz, and Neil feel more comfortable. Ask them to imagine they're sardines.*

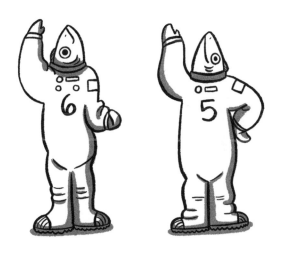

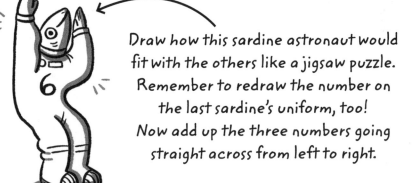

*Draw how this sardine astronaut would fit with the others like a jigsaw puzzle. Remember to redraw the number on the last sardine's uniform, too! Now add up the three numbers going straight across from left to right.*

*Need help? Turn to page 184.*

If you got a total of 20, turn to page 26.

Did you get 17? Go to page 18.

# MISSION COMMANDER PATH

Congratulations! NASA has made you the commander of this mission!

That means you're the astronaut in charge of the Apollo spacecraft on your six-day journey to the moon and back. The trip will be dangerous and challenging, so it's good that you've been training for this all your life.

In fact, in the early 1960s, you piloted jet planes that broke the speed of sound . . . like the one you can make on the next page.

Tear along the dotted lines to free the jet plane, and then fold it into shape like this: ⟶

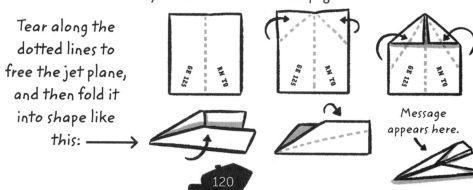

GE 125    RN TO

GE 125    RN TO

GE 125    RN TO

Message appears here.

**GE 125**

**RN TO**

When you're done, the words across the top of
the wings will tell you what to do next. If you get stuck
and need help,
flip to page 184.

In 1961, President John F. Kennedy challenged
the United States to put a person on the moon
by the end of the decade. As you watched
his speech on a black-and-white TV,
you thought, "I'll do it, Mr. President!"

PA

TU

"Let's go home this second!" you tell your surprised crewmates. Before they say anything, you burn valuable fuel turning your craft around and moving in the opposite direction.

Two hours later, the low-fuel alarm starts to blare. You have twenty minutes' worth of power left, and you're still two days away from Earth.

END

You need to find another way home! Go back to page 159.

The rocket's engines can be seen and felt miles away. And that's just where you are—miles away from the launch.

You forgot to put yourself onto the rocket. Your mission is over!

# END

I spy a better way to go. Turn to page 129 and try again!

Well done! Space in the command module is TIGHT. There's no room for a toilet. When you have to go number one, you'll use a special hose connected to the outside of the rocket. That's right—basically, you'll pee into space.

If you need to go number two, you'll use a plastic bag. Be sure to mix the special germicide into the bag when you're done. That will keep bacteria from growing inside the bag and causing it to explode! If that happened, everything would just kind of float around inside the cabin and—

*Ew. I can't keep talking about it. It's too much for me. Just imagine you're swimming in a pool—and someone drops a bag of popcorn into the water. Draw that scene here. That's kind of how everything from an exploded waste bag would float around in the cabin. When you're done, turn to page 146 . . . fast! I can't look!*

All those hours flying your plane and doing prep work have brought you to this day in the late 1960s. It's launch day! Today you'll blast off to the moon!

The sun isn't up yet, but you are. Technicians are helping you and two other astronauts, Fred Haise and Jack Swigert, get dressed in your space suits before you board the spaceship.

I've got GOOD news! Your 183-pound space suit and backpack will feel like only 30 pounds on the lunar surface— thanks to the moon's much lower gravity.

And now I've got BAD news.
Oh! Did I make you panic? I don't want to startle you!
To find out why, write these types of words in the blanks.

(a) adjective: _____

(b) adjective: _____

(c) vegetable: _____

(d) vegetable: _____

(e) topping for a hot dog: _____

When you're done, tear along the dotted line and fold over the flap!

OK, now you're ready for the bad news! Here it is:

Your nose itches.

I mean, it really, really ITCHES! Sealed inside your suit with your helmet on, you can't scratch your nose with your fingers. You definitely don't want to make an itchy-nose face right now—millions of people are watching you on TV, including your family and best friends.

*Go to the next page.*

*Use the words you just wrote to fill in the blanks!*

I'm glad you ate your favorite breakfast of _____ , _____
                                                (a)                            (b)

_____ , and _____ with _____ . I'd hate to startle
        (c)                             (d)                        (e)

you and make you spill food on your white pressure suit—it cost $100,000!

126

*Turn the page.*

I know what to do! Apollo 17 astronaut Harrison Schmitt was an expert at solving this problem. Can you guess how he scratched his nose? Draw your guess here. Then tear along the dotted lines and flip the flap up to see for yourself.

Oh, that's so much better. Now you can really enjoy the beautiful Florida weather as a van drives you and the two other astronauts eight miles from the preparation area to the launchpad. Your heart picks up speed when you spot the mammoth Saturn V rocket ahead. This three-part vehicle is the largest rocket ever built—363 feet tall. So there must be plenty of room for the crew inside, right?

*Go to the next page and follow the instructions on the corner flaps.*

Are you like Harrison? He stuck a piece of Velcro inside his helmet so he could he turn his head and scratch away. Itch your way to the next page!

128

Fold over this top corner first!

Fold over the bottom corner second!

129

Draw the crew here. Then fold over the bottom corner.

BUURRP!

Did you draw yourself on the rocket? Go to page 131.

Are you missing from your drawing? Flip to page 123.

130

You, Fred, and Jack will sit in the command module. That's a very small capsule on top of the Saturn V rocket.

An elevator will take you to the top. As you ride up, you can see through the cage wall of the elevator. Giant letters on the rocket seem to flash as you whiz past them:

S-E-T-A-T-S D-E-T-I-N-U

*Is that some kind of secret message?*
*Can you guess what it is?*
*Hint: Try reading it backward.*

The tanks inside the rocket are filled with supercooled liquid oxygen and hydrogen. The fuel is so cold that sheets of ice form on the sides of the rocket and peel off like skin from a snake. The rocket burps and moans and makes all sorts of strange noises.

*Draw a burping monster over here.*
*I really would like to see that.*
*When you're done, turn this page.*

131

Go to the next page.

At the top, you leave the elevator and walk across the platform to the command module. Crawling through the open hatch into the small compartment, you squeeze into the middle seat, between Fred and Jack.

*Clang!* The hatch swings shut and locks you inside.

But not to worry! The three of you won't be alone. Mission Control will be in touch with you about 99 percent of the time on the radio. That means hundreds of thousands of men and women will be working to make sure your trip is a success.

In fact, you can hear the booming voice of Mission Control counting down to launch right now:

"Ten, nine . . ."

Oh! I can barely stand the excitement. Each second takes you closer to blastoff!

"Eight, seven . . ."

What? Don't stop now! Keep the count going by
tearing along the dotted lines and folding up corner flap A.
Then follow the instructions.

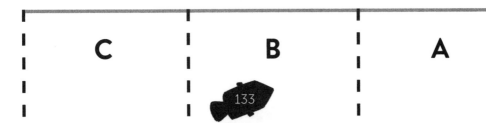

C     B     A

133

Party's over! Back to work!

In just a moment, your spacecraft will slam into Earth's upper atmosphere. Unlike outer space, our atmosphere is filled with "air"—so it will be a little like hitting a wall.

The command module is zinging through space at 25,000 miles per hour. That's fast enough to go back and forth between New York City and Los Angeles more than four times in an hour! Let me put it another way: On the highway your car usually goes about 88 feet per second. The command module is moving at **36,000** feet per second. Yikes!

You'll have to steer the command module so that you hit the atmosphere at just the right angle. If you come in too steep, the blunt force of the impact will tear the command module apart. If you enter the atmosphere too shallow, you'll skip along the top of it like a stone over the surface of a pool—and you'll completely miss Earth.

*You won't be able to see the path you'll take into the atmosphere from inside the capsule. Show you can trust your instincts. Close your eyes and draw a line through the path. Keep trying until you can do it without touching the sides. When you do, turn to page 161.*

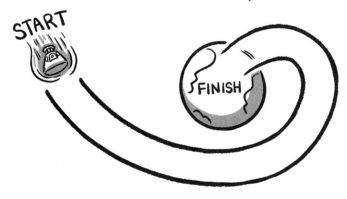

Fold up flap B.

... Three

Fold up flap C.

... Two

Turn to page 81.

... One

On the Apollo 8 mission, astronaut William Anders snapped a photo called *Earthrise*. The picture changed many people's lives. For the first time, they saw how tiny Earth looks from outer space. It made them realize that everyone on Earth should be working together to protect our planet.

*Draw your own <u>Earthrise</u> here. Turn over the corner flap when you're done to compare your photo with William Anders's pic.*

Your computer asks you to pick a card. And then it announces it will pull a rabbit from a hat right after it saws its assistant in half.

Apparently, you've misprogrammed your computer. It couldn't care less about getting back to Earth. Instead, its biggest dream is to be a magician!

Abracadabra . . . the mission is over!

# END

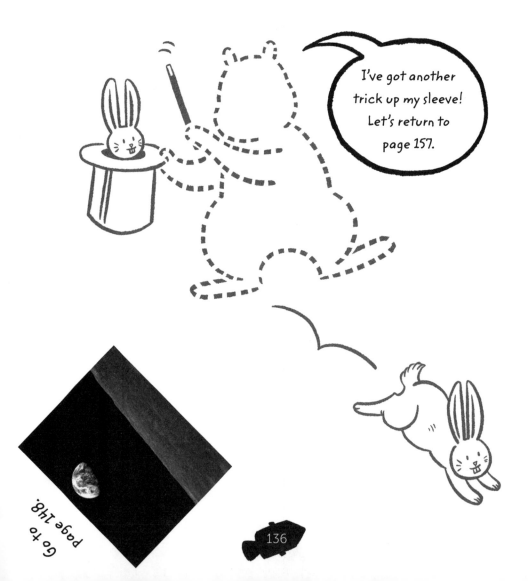

I've got another trick up my sleeve! Let's return to page 157.

Go to page 148.

Superb! In between bouncing around the capsule, you rearranged your spacecraft modules. Your service module is now connected to your command module, which is docked with the lunar module. You're ready to land on the moon . . . but you won't arrive there for two days.

"We've got time," Fred says. "I might as well unleash one of my famous knock-knock jokes."

*Oh no. I've heard about his knock-knock jokes. They're horrible!*

*BLAM!!* The entire spacecraft jolts violently.

"What was that?" Jack asks nervously when things go quiet again.

You can't answer him.

But I can. There was an explosion in the service module. (I promise I didn't do it to stop Fred's joke.)

*Tear along the dotted line and fold this flap up to see for yourself.*

Uh-oh. Turn to page 51.

Turn the page.

138

Wait. Where are YOU? Because I can't see you on the moon, I'm just going to assume you're inside a volcano on the distant planet of Januso. Have fun!

# END

I just **lava** happy ending! Let's go back to page 76 and try again.

The power of the rocket and the speed you're traveling at press you into your seat and push your cheeks back.

PAGE 176

*The first stage of the rocket runs out of fuel and falls away. It will tumble into the ocean below. Once the second stage of the rocket empties of fuel, it drops off, too.*

Welcome to Earth orbit! You'll be here just long enough to catch your breath and take off your helmet.

"We're really on our way to the moon, guys!" you announce, and share high fives with your crew.

The command module (CM) and the service module (SM) will travel as a single unit—called the command service module (CSM)—for much of your journey.

*Go to the next page.*

Since you're going to live here for the next six days,
draw a picture of everything you'll need.
Think about every room (and I mean **every** kind of room!)
in your house that you would visit in a day.

When you're done, fold over the flap.

Wonderful. So you have a toilet on board! *That's great news,* you think as you take advantage of this wonderful convenience.

Or . . . is it? Without gravity, liquids and solids won't stay put in a bowl and will FLOAT in the air.

The radio crackles and you hear: "This is Mission Control. We're detecting massive errors on the craft. Are you seeing any alarm lights?"

Just then, an alarm sounds and lights flash on the panel in front of you. Uh-oh.

Fred and Jack exchange nervous looks. But you're the boss, and you try to keep calm. "Jack, can you tell what's going on?"

After checking the alarm codes, Jack says, "For some reason, all major systems behind one panel are failing. What do you want to do, Commander?"

## Go to the next page.

Did you draw a toilet? Yes—turn the page. No—turn to page 124.

I'm not even going to bother giving you a choice.
Quick! Find out what's happening.
Draw a screwdriver turning this screw.
Now tear along the dotted lines and fold the page
back to open the panel and look inside it on page 145.

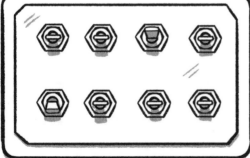

Aces! You're ready to power down the CSM for now and board the LM. It's going to be VERY tight. Good thing the three of you are great friends!

I don't know about you, but all this excitement has made me a bit sleepy. The LM is usually used by only two astronauts, and they put up hammocks, one over the other, in order to get some sleep.

*Where will you put the third hammock*
*so you can get some shut-eye, too?*
*Draw it here, and then go to page 158.*

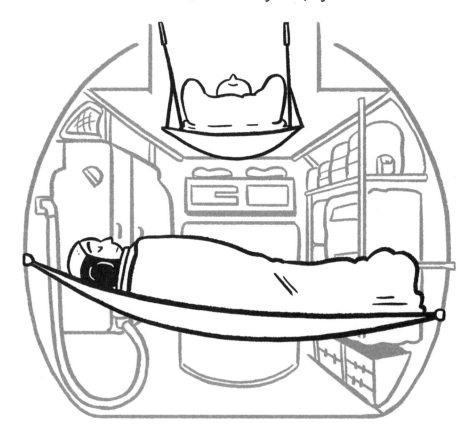

Those are yellow droplets of liquid, aren't they? Something similar happened on the Project Mercury flight in 1963.

Now, where could that liquid have come from? Don't answer that! It's too disgusting! I'm shutting this mission down!

# END

Let's do a redo (do). Flip back to page 141 and go again.

Okay, now that you're a little lighter . . . you can enjoy being lighter! You're experiencing the near-zero gravity of space. There's not a lot of room in this tiny module, but you and your crewmates can still have fun floating around and bouncing off the walls.

*Things are about to get very tricky, so you'd better have a good time now!*

Connect the dots to complete each astronaut's bouncy path.
The three shapes you draw will look like numbers.
Use those three numbers to fill in the blanks.

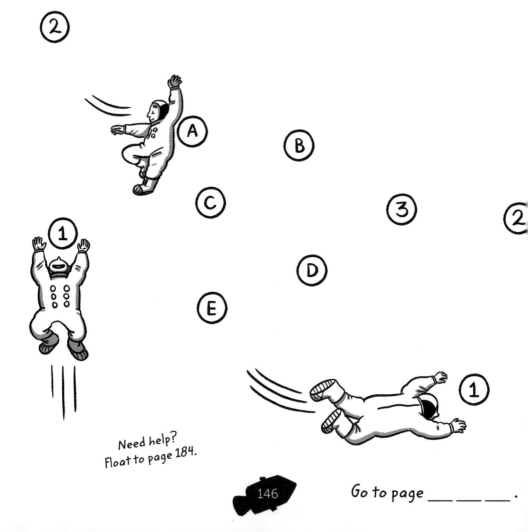

Need help?
Float to page 184.

Go to page ___ ___ ___ .

So you think 1202 is a scary number? You know what might be even worse? Have you heard of pi? It goes on forever . . . just like the regret you have for giving up your mission too soon!

# END

Let's take on 1202!
Return to page 55.

Just then the radio crackles, and static has never sounded so good.

"Apollo, uh, this is Houston," Mission Control says with a little hesitation. "Welcome back to full communication. . . ."

Your spacecraft has emerged from the moon's shadow. Then why does Mission Control sound so nervous?

"We're getting signals from your ship again, and they're not good," Mission Control explains. "The carbon dioxide in your spacecraft is climbing to dangerous levels."

Oh no! Did you know that each time you breathe, you release a gas called carbon dioxide? It is harmless in small quantities, but at high levels, it's deadly. The filters on the spaceship are supposed to remove the gas.

So why are the levels rising? The filter in the LM is only meant to clean the air for two people . . . not three people! And there aren't any more filters.

Soon you and your crew will grow dizzy. Three hours after that you'll be . . . well, let's just say my friend Amicus will be making a visit.

*Go to the next page.*

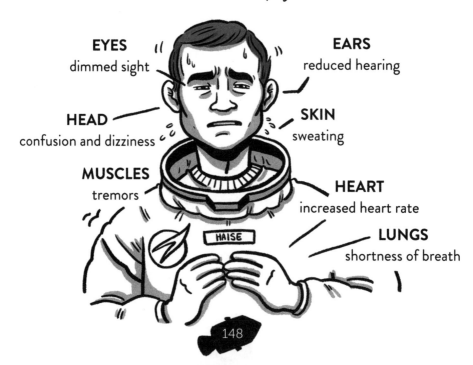

EYES
dimmed sight

EARS
reduced hearing

HEAD
confusion and dizziness

SKIN
sweating

MUSCLES
tremors

HEART
increased heart rate

HAISE

LUNGS
shortness of breath

T S U R H D M
S N E E T A U
O K A Y T E S
H R I E E H C
T S G N U L L
E A R S N E E
X T P A G E S

Oh! I hate to have to tell you all the symptoms
you'll soon have! So I'll just show you.
In the word search, circle the **BOLDFACED** word from
each of the seven labels on the astronaut on page 148.
Write the leftover letters in order in these blanks.
They will spell out what to do next!

\_\_\_\_\_ \_\_ \_\_\_ \_\_\_\_ \_\_\_\_

Need help?
Turn to page 184.

"Mission Control, I have an idea," you say. "Do we have what we need to make our own filter up here? That way we could clean the air of carbon dioxide."

"Yes!" Mission Control answers. "We were thinking the same thing! Our team has reviewed all 445 pieces of equipment on your craft, and we've come up with a way to make a filter. You need to find five items . . . FAST!"

On page 151 are the names of five objects that Mission Control tells you to find. Draw each item next to its name when you spot it in the picture below. The pair of scissors is easy—I've circled it and drawn it for you—but the rest of the list is tricky.

The crew of Apollo 13 was able to find these items! Can you? If you need a hint, tear along the lines and turn over the flap next to the name of the item. When you've found and drawn all the items, tear along the dotted lines and fold down this top flap.

Scissors

Cardboard

Plastic bag

Duct tape

Extra hose

151

Turn to page 168.

Time to judge a book by its cover . . . cardboard cover, that is! The lunar landing manual has a cardboard cover.

Oops! I can only think of two things to say right now. One, you didn't untangle the parachutes. And, two . . .
*WHAM!*

# END

The long underwear you were going to wear on the moon is in the plastic bag.

I know a third thing to say: Let's return to page 161 and try that again!

Duct tape is stowed on every mission. Look in the open cabinet.

See that space suit? It's not making use of the hose right now.

What a fantastic gas station! Unfortunately, it will be at least a few decades before that station can be built. And you definitely can't wait that long. You'd better work with Mission Control to fix your problem.

"One of the oxygen tanks in the service module exploded," Mission Control tells you. "You'll have enough oxygen until you get back to Earth, but only if you save it when you can. Otherwise . . ."

*Hmm. I've never been good at holding my breath.*
*What will you do next?*

Go outside to
fix the problem?
Turn to page 33.

Retreat into the
lunar module?
Go to page 156.

"Roger that," Alex says when he receives your message. "Rebooting the computer now."

Seconds later, the alarm lights stop blinking and—*phew!*—the guidance system is working the way it should. The rocket continues to climb! Aces! But there's no time to celebrate. It's still over 200,000 miles to the moon.

The rest of the flight plan can be a little *puzzling*, to say the least. Let's make sure you know how the pieces of your journey fit together.

*Good luck! Turn to page 34!*

Okay! That was very childish of YOU. I'm shocked a commander would dream up that activity. Just shocked!

*Okay, okay, I might have had a little something to do with it.*

You'll be coming out from behind the moon soon—and when you do, you're going to want to capture the view. Quick! Get a camera!

Oh, looks like Fred is already using the camera NASA put on board.

Good thing NASA allows each astronaut to bring a little cloth drawstring bag on the mission with small personal mementos, like family photos or a charm. Are you carrying your own camera in your Personal Preference Kit?

PAGE 179

**What two things would you put in your Personal Preference Kit? Draw them here, and then fold over the flap.**

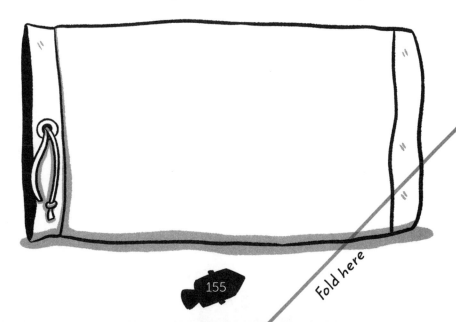

Fold here

Yes! Ships on the ocean have lifeboats that passengers can use. Why shouldn't a ship in space have one, too?

You were supposed to use the lunar module once you reached the moon. But you can turn the lunar module into a kind of lifeboat now! If the three of you travel in the smaller LM, you'll save power and oxygen. That's what the crew of Apollo 13 did!

Before you leave the command module, though, you need to shut it down so you can use its power later. That means turning off the computer.

*The phone you might have in your pocket right now is millions of times more powerful than the Apollo mission computer.*

When you turn off the computer, it will forget pretty much everything. So first you're going to need to program the LM's computer with all the information that was on the CM's.

*Are you good at coding? Prove it!*
*1. Finish the drawing of the spacebot here.*
*2. Now move it where the code instructs.*
*3. What number did you land on?*
*Use it to fill in the blank.*

Go to page _____.

**CODE:**           <u>CODE KEY</u>

□    □    ◉    ◖

   __    __    __    __

□ = Up 1

◖ = Down 2

◆ = Left 2

◉ = Right 2

Did you draw a comet? No? Go back and add it! Yes? Get clicking and go to page 155.

156

| 136 | 144 | 136 |
| 144 | 136 | 144 |
| 136 | 144 | 136 |
|  | 136 | 144 |

START

157

Now that you've had a nap, I think you're ready to hear this message from Mission Control.

"Your spacecraft is too damaged to attempt a moon landing," Mission Control tells you. "We're all very sorry down here on Earth. You won't be walking on the moon during this trip."

Oh! You take in the news. All that training you went through. All that preparation. It's tough to accept that a moon landing won't happen—but you still have to figure out how to get home! You'd better handle those feelings before you move on.

Draw a horrible-feelings monster here, and lock it
in this cage so you can hide from your disappointment.
When you're done, tear along the dotted line,
fold over the flap, and follow the instructions.

DO NOT FEED!

Hmm. The only headway we seem to be making is straight down!

# END

Let's make things right.
Return to page 169.

Surprise! You can't hide from your feelings. Or from HUGE decisions like this. You have to make a choice. I highly recommend that you flip to my Escapologist Files. Or you can just wing it. Either way, good luck!

PAGE
181

Will you stop and head home right now?
Turn to page 122.

Or will you continue on your way to the moon?
Turn to page 92.

As your capsule rubs against Earth's atmosphere, a LOT of heat is created. You turn the spacecraft so that your heat shields are taking the brunt of the friction. You're 400,000 feet above the planet's surface and going so fast that the outside of the capsule bursts into flames.

*You're a meteor falling through the sky!*

The atmosphere has slowed you down—but you're still traveling at over 300 miles per hour. If you hit the ocean at this speed, the 11,000-pound command module will be smashed to smithereens.

PAGE 178

*Time to release the parachutes! Oops. They're all tangled!*

*Which line leads to the parachutes?*
*Follow it—then follow the directions!*

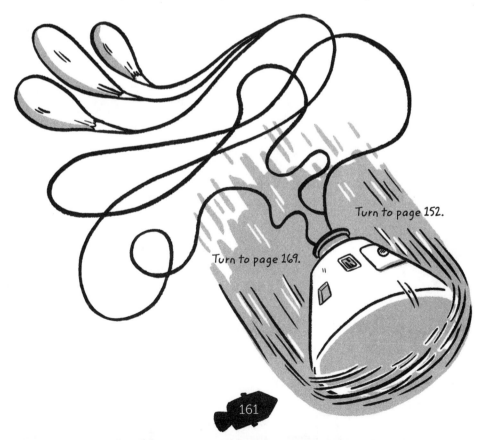

Turn to page 152.

Turn to page 169.

You've picked a spot to land, and the LM continues to fall as fast as an elevator moves. You must be close to the surface—you can't be sure. The rocket blast is whipping up moondust and making it tricky for you to see.

"You have ten seconds' worth of fuel left," Mission Control says over the radio. "If you can't land soon, you'll have to abort the landing."

Time is running out. Your gaze goes to the control panel, where a blue light starts flashing.

Alan sees the light, too, and turns to you with wide eyes.

This is what Mission Control told Neil Armstrong and Buzz Aldrin during Apollo 11!

Oh! I'm too anxious to look at him!
Draw his mouth, nose, and eyebrows on page 163.

Does he seem happy and excited?
Go to page 97.

Or scared and worried?
Turn to page 94.

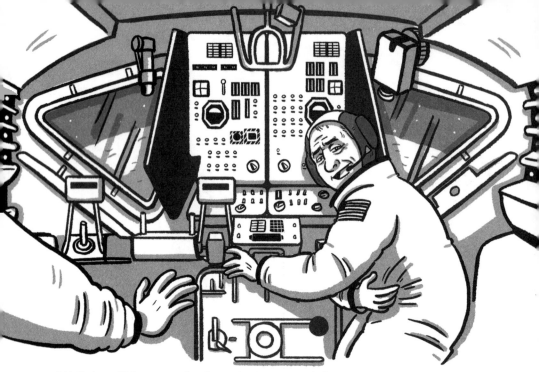

Well done! You zoom back to the lunar module.

You jump off the moon buggy, rush on board, and quickly remove your backpack, gloves, and helmet. Poor Alan is slumped over and weak.

"We're going to leave now and get you to that medicine on the CSM," you tell him. "Don't worry!"

"What's there to worry about?" Alan jokes in a weak whisper.

Just then Mission Control calls your name. "The switch to arm the engine is on open. That means you won't be able to turn on the engine. What's going on up there?"

Um, how do I tell you this VERY bad news? When you were rushing around, the backpack on your suit must have hit the control panel, and something snapped off.

And that something is the switch that turns on the engine.

If you can't fire up the engine, you and Alan will never leave the moon.

"What's that you said about not worrying?" Alan asks, this time a little more seriously.

164

*Go to page 117.*

*Ugh. It's just like that movie. No one wants to be here!*
*As you go around the moon, it's waaaayyyy too quiet.*
*It's like being in a library made of pillows!*

Your crewmates are feeling it, too. The silence is just adding to the stress.
Finally Jack suggests, "Let's tie on the feed bags!"

Great idea! Even with everything going on, you still need to eat.

*Mission Control wants astronauts to eat 2,800 calories a day.*

You open a cabinet and pull out a bag of beef with vegetables. To keep bacteria from destroying your food, it's been freeze-dried. That means all the moisture was sucked out before the food was sealed in the plastic bag.

Strap the bag to your suit with Velcro so it doesn't float away in the low gravity. Now grab the water gun off the wall and insert it into the bag's nozzle to add water. Then squeeze the food into your mouth through the flat tube.

*Yuck! Is there a pizza parlor on board?*

The liquid makes the food in the bag soupy. Hmm. You know what this goopy gunk would be perfect for? Can you guess?

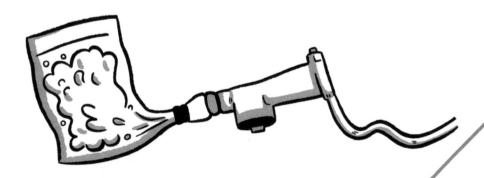

*I have two words for you.*
*Fold up the flap. Then go on to the next page.*

Face off in the ultimate space food battle!

**How to play:** For each turn, you will flip a coin.

If you get **HEADS,** it's either Jack's or Fred's turn (you choose each time). Have one of them squirt you with cottage cheese or tuna fish. Each time you get squirted, color in a bubble above your head. That bubble is popped!

If you get **TAILS,** it's your turn! Squirt your beef with vegetables at either Fred or Jack. Each time you splat one of them, color in a bubble above that crewmate's head.

Once all three bubbles above a player's head are filled in, the game is finished. If your three bubbles pop before Jack's or Fred's, try again!

When you succeed in popping all of Jack's or Fred's bubbles, go to page 155.

JACK

YOU

FRED

FOOD FIGHT!

166

Brilliant! With the filter in place, I can breathe easier already. *Literally.*

While you've been working, your craft has been hurtling through space. You're just about 70 minutes away from Earth. So close! But I'm still worried you're going to run out of air.

Wanting to save as much of the command module's power as possible, you stay in the lunar module until the last second.

"We can't wait any longer," you tell Jack and Fred, and you lead the way back into the command module. Once Jack closes the hatch that connects the CM to the LM, you undock it.

The LM floats away. It will fall through Earth's atmosphere, where it will burn up.

Let's throw a going-away party.
Draw a party for the LM here. Then turn to page 134.

Aces! As Mission Control radios instructions, you spend about an hour putting everything together.

The cardboard covers support the plastic and create a box shape. The hose is attached to the box. The tape, which you cut with the scissors, keeps your makeshift filter from leaking.

Put the puzzle pieces together.
When you do, follow the directions you make!
You want your new filter to look like the one
that the crew of the Apollo 13 mission built:

If you get stuck, flip to page 184.

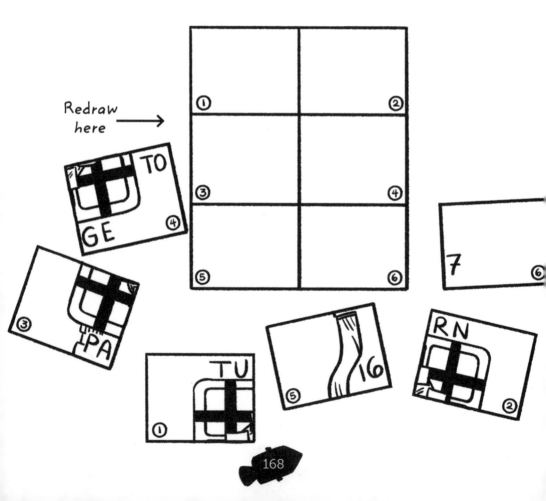

Redraw here →

Well done! You've reduced your speed to a pleasant 20 miles per hour, and you splash down gently into the South Pacific Ocean.

*Ahh! Nothing like a little dip after a long trip.*

You just traveled 541,103 miles over six days on a very dangerous journey through space, but your adventure isn't over. You still have to escape this capsule!

Um, what's going on? Did Earth's gravity flip while you were gone?

Oh! That's right. About half the Apollo missions ended with the capsule rolling upside down once it hit the water—leaving the astronauts hanging in their seat belts.

Luckily, the capsule is equipped with righting spheres . . . flotation balls that can make things right!

*If you had to attach the righting spheres, where would you put them?*

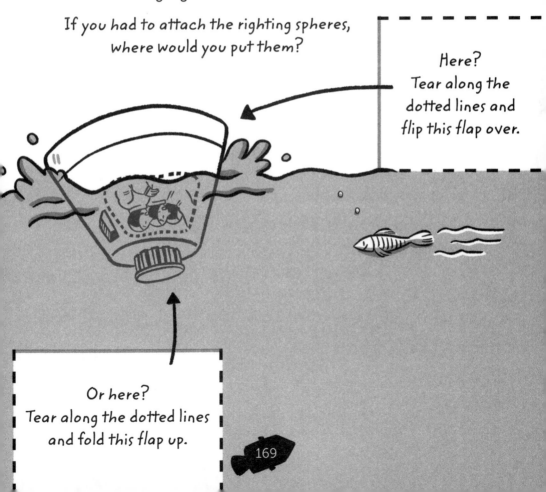

*Here?*
*Tear along the dotted lines and flip this flap over.*

*Or here?*
*Tear along the dotted lines and fold this flap up.*

Turn to page 160.

170

Go to page 171.

"Here comes the recovery team!" Jack points out the window. Up in the sky, something is zipping toward you.

It's a US Navy helicopter from the nearby recovery ship!

The helicopter swoops down and drops US Navy swimmers into the water. They attach a circular raft around the outside of the command module. That will block water from rushing inside when the hatch is opened. A swimmer climbs up on the raft and taps on the door. *Knock-knock.*

"Who's there?" Frank says, and you all burst out laughing.

As the swimmer swings open the hatch, fresh air rushes inside. After being cooped up for six days with two people in a tiny capsule. . . . ohhhhh! You've never smelled anything so sweet.

*Or maybe you have! Draw it on page 170.*
*When you're done, turn the page.*

Well done! You've made your escape!
Countries around the world are
hosting parades in your honor.

Track your progress as you finish escaping in each
of the three roles by drawing yourself
into the scene and drawing a section
of the patch below for each path.

Draw the mission
commander here.

Draw the moon
buggy driver here.

MISSION PATCH

Moon Buggy Driver

Flight Director

Mission Commander

WELCOME BACK, ASTRONAUTS

Draw the flight director here.

I have a secret to share . . . but only with someone who has the potential to be a great escapologist. Prove you're that someone by completing ALL THREE paths that start on page 7. When you've done that—and only then!—turn to page 174.

# CONGRATULATIONS!

You have proven yourself worthy. You're one step closer to becoming my assistant and perhaps someday—maybe!—a Master Escapologist.

Now, as promised, I will reveal more about myself. This might be hard for you to believe because you know how talented I am. But I am actually locked in a room right now . . . and I cannot get out. That is why I need an assistant.

If you keep your escapes great (like mine), someday we will meet!


*Evolo Cherishwise,*
*Master Escapologist*


PS My last name is actually an anagram of someone who's very well known and who shares pursuits similar to mine. Do you know who it is?

# ESCAPOLOGIST FILES

## From the Desk of the Master Escapologist

I'm sad to say that NASA didn't hire many women in the 1960s and '70s. During the Apollo era, at least 95 percent of the workers at NASA were men. Yes, incredible women worked there, including JoAnn Morgan—the only woman in Mission Control during Apollo 11—and Poppy Northcutt—an engineer who helped guide the Apollo 13 crew back to Earth after an explosion rocked their spacecraft. But it's very unlikely that Lynette (a character I made up!) would have been running simulations at this time. In later years, NASA made an effort to narrow the gap at the space agency and began hiring more women.

To add to the excitement of your escape, I've lumped jobs at Apollo Mission Control together under four main categories. For instance, I've combined **booster systems engineer** and **retrofire officer** under the title **rocket controller**. And I've tucked **electrical, environmental, and communications controller (EECOM)** into **systems check**. These larger categories will make it easier for me to keep firing off challenges—and I won't get bogged down in the nitty-gritty!

### Fast Fact!
The moon has one-sixth the gravity of Earth—everything and everyone feels lighter there!

AAHHHHHH!

*This machine helped prepare astronauts for the incredible forces they would experience during blastoff. They hated how dizzy and awful the machine made them feel—but it might make an interesting birthday present for a friend!*

## 🎖 Medal Magazine 🎖

Want to win a NASA exceptional service medal? Then do something like technician Jack Garman did! Just before the launch of Apollo 11, he wrote down all the different alarm codes that the lunar module's computer might generate—and how NASA should respond to each one. So when the code 1202 flashed on his screen and a split-second decision had to be made, Jack just checked his list. He knew instantly that the mission should continue. NASA awarded him the medal for his quick thinking and for NOT aborting the mission.

# FASHION RECALL!

All astronauts should stop wearing the NASA urine collection device from 1963! Astronaut Gordon Cooper discovered the device's flaw when his Project Mercury test flight started to go terribly wrong. The systems in his one-person spacecraft began to fail toward the end of his 34-hour mission—for no apparent reason. Luckily, he was able to manually reenter the atmosphere and land safely, but just barely. Back on Earth, NASA discovered the reason for all the headaches: Gordon's urine bag had leaked, and drops of urine had gotten into all the wiring!

## CAN I QUOTE YOU?

In a famous movie, an actor playing an Apollo 13 astronaut says, "Houston, we have a problem." But in real life, astronaut James Lovell said, "Houston, we've had a problem." Can you spot the difference?

**persist *(verb)*:** to continue on a course of action despite difficulty
EXAMPLE: *Stu Roosa, the command module pilot on Apollo 14, persisted. While trying to dock the CM with the LM, Stu couldn't get the drogue to latch onto the probe—the command ship and the lunar craft kept bouncing away from each other. He tried going slow and then fast . . . but nothing seemed to work. He didn't give up, though, and finally, after almost two hours, they connected! (NASA concluded that a piece of dirt or grime might have interfered.)*

## Now Offering . . . NASA Lingo Lessons!

Embarrassed that all your friends know the latest NASA lingo and you don't? Now's your chance to be part of the cool crowd! Learn all the jargon, like . . .

**CM:** command module
**CSM:** command service module
**LM:** lunar module
**S/C:** spacecraft
**EVA:** extravehicular activity (anything astronauts do outside the spacecraft)

On July 21, 1969, Neil Armstrong and Buzz Aldrin performed the first EVA on the lunar surface— a moonwalk!

## One Small Pen, One Giant Solution

After a successful mission, Apollo 11's Neil Armstrong and Buzz Aldrin prepared to leave the moon. Buzz was using a pen to take notes, when he noticed that either he or Neil must have bumped into the LM's control panel—the switch to arm the engine for takeoff had broken off! They might be stranded on the moon! Buzz didn't panic. He realized that the answer to their problem was in his hand: He could use the pen to activate the circuit breaker!

## Infographic Magazine

While there was never a tangle of parachute lines on missions to the moon, Apollo 15 did experience a main-parachute failure. This parachute went flat. These two stayed open, and the capsule splashed down safely.

Each parachute had a half acre of fabric.

Two million stitches in the fabric prevented tears.

Each parachute had suspension lines that were a mile and a half long.

Great care was given to packing these enormous parachutes. It took a week to fold and store each one.

# WEIGHT FOR IT!*

Did you know . . . ?
A human baby weighs about 8 pounds.
A baby African elephant weighs about 200 pounds.
A baby blue whale weighs about 6,000 pounds.

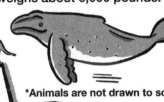

*Animals are not drawn to scale.

## On This Day in Underpants

During a NASA training mission, the crew had to remove their undergarments. Why? Their underwear was giving off lithium fluorine—a poisonous gas!

## Who Brought What?

On Apollo 11, astronaut Michael Collins included three flags in his Personal Preference Kit: the flags of the United States, the District of Columbia, and the US Air Force.

Your carry-on items must fit in here! →

# LIGHTNING NEVER STRIKES TWICE

Apollo 12's Saturn V rocket was struck by lightning twice—once at 36 seconds after liftoff and again at 52 seconds. There was some damage to the spacecraft's systems, but the mission was not aborted.

EVA stands for "extravehicular activity."

Dear EVA Pro, ????

I'm headed out on an Apollo mission. Can I go outside the ship while we're traveling in space?

Signed,
Don't Know Apollo

## DEAR DON'T KNOW,

Sure, but make certain you're prepared for the toughest walk of your life! Just ask astronaut Gene Cernan. He tried going outside his traveling ship while on a Gemini mission—before the Apollo missions. Gene's heart started beating too fast, his heavy breathing fogged up his helmet, and he had a tricky time getting back into the spacecraft! So I'd recommend staying inside a traveling spacecraft and saving your walking for the moon!

Sincerely yours,
EVA Pro

## PEOPLE VS. COMPUTERS

During the Apollo 11 mission, the lunar module's computer began acting up. Neil Armstrong took over the controls while his crewmate Buzz Aldrin described the dwindling fuel levels and altitude. Neil chose to continue flying over a giant crater and a boulder field in order to find a safer spot to land.

## Bird-Word Watchers

I'm often asked, "What's your favorite bird quote?" The answer is easy! When Neil Armstrong brought the lunar module safely to the moon's surface, he proclaimed to the whole world, "The *Eagle* has landed."

## ☑ WAYS TO WATCH THE MOON LANDING

When Apollo 11's Neil Armstrong takes his first step on the moon, it will certainly be the biggest TV moment of the century! Don't have a TV? Here are a few places to watch: a friend's house, an airport, or even an appliance store!

*Sears department stores tuned all their TVs to the moon landing so customers could watch the historic event!*

# MEET NASA HEROES

Before electronic computers could perform calculations at lightning speeds, "human computers"—NASA mathematicians—spent hours, days, or weeks on a single calculation to make sure the numbers were just right. Their answers would help determine flight paths, space maneuvers, and other Apollo mission activities. Astronauts' lives were at stake. These three women were among those human computers, who didn't always get the recognition they deserved for their intelligence and ingenuity, which helped fuel our nation's exploration of space.

**KATHERINE JOHNSON**    **DOROTHY VAUGHAN**    **MARY JACKSON**

# THE BIG QUESTION

You're on the Apollo 13 mission. You've just had an explosion on your CSM halfway to the moon, and you've been told that you can't land on the lunar surface. What do you do?

☐ Stop and go home?

☑ Continue to the moon?

The Apollo 13 team decided to continue on toward the moon instead of turning directly back to Earth.

# ADDITIONAL EXPLORING

Here are a few of the sources the Master Escapologist
used for research when putting together this adventure.

## BOOKS

Graham, Ian. *Space Travel e.guide.* New York: DK Publishing, 2004.

Morgan, Ben, ed. *Space! The Universe as You've Never Seen It Before!*
New York: DK Publishing, 2015.

Paris, Stephanie. *20th Century: Race to the Moon.*
Huntington Beach, CA: Teacher Created Materials, 2013.

Wilkinson, Philip. *Spacebusters: The Race to the Moon.*
New York: DK Publishing, 2012.

Zoehfeld, Kathleen Weidner. *Apollo 13* (Totally True Adventures).
New York: Random House Children's Books, 2015.

## WEBSITES

Holland, Brynn. "Human Computers: The Women of NASA." History.
Updated August 22, 2018. history.com/news/human-computers-women-at-nasa.

NASA. "From Hidden to Modern Figures."
Last updated June 12, 2019. nasa.gov/modernfigures/overview.

NASA. "Mission Control at NASA Johnson Space Center:
History and Restoration." July 16, 2019. YouTube video, 3:02:30.
youtube.com/watch?v=v8aWXJeh9R4.

NASA. "Space Educators' Handbook: Kids' Space."
Last updated May 23, 2012. er.jsc.nasa.gov/seh/kidspace.htm.

# ANSWERS

p. 8: Mystery Phrase: A TO B

p. 15: Turn to page TWENTY-FOUR.

p. 35: Turn to page THIRTY-seven.

p. 73: Turn to page 75.

p. 83: Go to page 86.

p. 92: Turn to page 116.

p. 107: Turn to page 91.

p. 114: TURN TO PAGE 164.

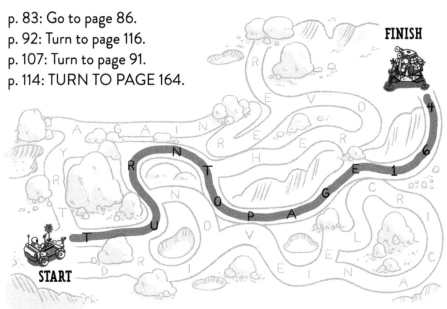

p. 119: The correct answer is 20.

6 + 9 + 5 = 20

p. 121: The wings of the plane should reveal this: TURN TO PAGE 125.
p. 146: Go to page 137.
p. 148: TURN TO THE NEXT PAGE.

p. 149:

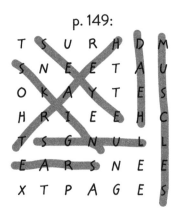

p. 168: Image will reveal TURN TO PAGE 167.

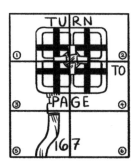

# BILL DOYLE

Bill Doyle is the author of <u>Escape This Book! Titanic,</u> <u>Escape This</u> <u>Book! Tombs of Egypt,</u> <u>Attack of the Shark-Headed Zombie,</u> and <u>Behind Enemy Lines,</u> as well as many other books for kids—with over two million copies in print. He has also created lots of games for Sesame Workshop, Warner Bros., and Nerf. He says, "My happiest moment as an author was when the genius Master Escapologist sent me a secret message offering me the job to write his incredible books." (No, he's not just saying that because the Master Escapologist is writing this biography!) Bill lives in New York City.

BillDoyleBooks.com

# MASTER ESCAPOLOGIST

Let me put it this way—you don't get named a Master Escapologist unless you are the best . . . and that is exactly what I am. THE BEST! I'm not going to give you any hints here about my true identity. You'll have to make your escape in this book to discover more about me!

# SARAH SAX

Sarah Sax is an illustrator and comic artist based in Portland, Maine. She studied illustration, animation, and storytelling at Hampshire College and has a background in arts education. Sarah cares deeply about how, why, and what people create, and she works to foster the creative spark in makers of all ages.

SarahSax.me

# Make your next
# GREAT ESCAPE!

Doodle, decide, and demolish
your way off the <u>Titanic</u> or
out of an ancient tomb!